Coco Crazy . . .

Brooke's mom went to the stereo and put on a tape. Then she turned to Brooke. "I'm excited to see your reaction," she said.

Brooke sat on the edge of the sofa eagerly listening for the results of her mom's new singing career. She'd heard her mom sing before, of course, but not since she was a little kid, and then her mom had sung mostly lullabies. She had no idea what kind of songs her mother sang now. Golden oldies? Folk music? Jazz? Rhythm and blues?

But what she heard was so incredible that at first she couldn't believe it. What she heard was the throaty, sexy sound of Coco singing "Chocolate Kisses for My Baby"!

"Mom," she whispered incredulously. "Are you sure you put on the right tape?"

"That's me, honey," her mom said.

"That's you? I don't believe it!" Brooke exclaimed. "You're Coco!"

D1388620

SWEET VALLEY TWINS titles, published by Bantam Books.
Ask your bookseller for titles you have missed:

1. BEST FRIENDS
2. TEACHER'S PET
3. THE HAUNTED HOUSE
4. CHOOSING SIDES
5. SNEAKING OUT
6. THE NEW GIRL
7. THREE'S A CROWD
8. FIRST PLACE
9. AGAINST THE RULES
10. ONE OF THE GANG
11. BURIED TREASURE
12. KEEPING SECRETS
13. STRETCHING THE TRUTH
14. TUG OF WAR
17. BOYS AGAINST GIRLS
18. CENTRE OF ATTENTION
19. THE BULLY
20. PLAYING HOOKY
21. LEFT BEHIND
32. JESSICA ON STAGE
33. ELIZABETH'S NEW HERO
34. JESSICA, THE ROCK STAR

37. THE WAR BETWEEN THE TWINS
38. LOIS STRIKES BACK
39. JESSICA AND THE MONEY
    MIX-UP
40. DANNY MEANS TROUBLE
41. THE TWINS GET CAUGHT
42. JESSICA'S SECRET
43. ELIZABETH'S FIRST KISS
44. AMY MOVES IN
45. LUCY TAKES THE REINS
46. MADEMOISELLE JESSICA
47. JESSICA'S NEW LOOK
48. MANDY MILLER FIGHTS BACK
49. THE TWINS' LITTLE SISTER
50. JESSICA AND THE SECRET STAR
51. ELIZABETH THE IMPOSSIBLE
52. BOOSTER BOYCOTT
53. THE SLIME THAT ATE SWEET
    VALLEY
54. THE BIG PARTY WEEKEND
55. BROOKE AND HER ROCK-STAR
    MUM

SWEET VALLEY TWINS SUPER CHILLERS

1. THE CHRISTMAS GHOST
2. THE GHOST IN THE GRAVEYARD
3. THE CARNIVAL GHOST

SWEET VALLEY TWINS SUPER EDITIONS

1. THE CLASS TRIP
3. THE BIG CAMP SECRET
4. THE UNICORNS GO HAWAIIAN

SWEET VALLEY TWINS

Brooke and Her Rock-Star Mum

Written by
Jamie Suzanne

Created by
FRANCINE PASCAL

BANTAM BOOKS
TORONTO · NEW YORK · LONDON · SYDNEY · AUCKLAND

BROOKE AND HER ROCK-STAR MUM
A BANTAM BOOK 0 553 40457 1

Originally published in U.S.A. by Bantam Skylark Books

First publication in Great Britain

PRINTING HISTORY
Bantam edition published 1992
Sweet Valley High® and Sweet Valley Twins are registered
trademarks of Francine Pascal.

Conceived by Francine Pascal.

Produced by Daniel Weiss Associates, Inc., 33 West 17th Street,
New York, NY 10011

Bantam Books are published by Transworld Publishers Ltd.,
61–63 Uxbridge Road, Ealing, London W5 5SA, in Australia by
Transworld Publishers (Australia) Pty. Ltd., 15–23 Helles Avenue,
Moorebank, NSW 2170, and in New Zealand by Transworld
Publishers (N.Z.) Ltd., 3 William Pickering Drive, Albany,
Auckland.

Printed and bound in Great Britain by
Cox & Wyman Ltd., Reading

To the children of Rosie and Harry's Place

One

◇

"Hey, Elizabeth," Jessica Wakefield said as she came into her twin sister's bedroom Monday after school. "Look who's here."

"Hi, Brooke," Elizabeth Wakefield said, turning down the volume on her radio.

"Hey, Elizabeth," Brooke said. "I was wondering if you could help me come up with an idea for my *Sixers* 'Meet the Stars' article. Jessica's already doing Johnny Buck, you're doing Nick England, and Mandy's doing Donny Diamond. How many other stars are there to meet?" Brooke smiled. With her long wavy brown hair and fashionable clothing, Brooke Dennis looked like she'd just stepped off the cover of *Teenager* magazine.

Since she had moved to Sweet Valley many months before, she had become one of Elizabeth's closest friends. Jessica liked her, too, in spite of the fact that Brooke had refused to join the Unicorns, the exclusive club at Sweet Valley Middle School to which Jessica belonged.

Elizabeth laughed. "Sit down. We'll think of somebody."

Brooke sat down on the floor next to Elizabeth. "I was surprised not to see any signs of the party when I came up the stairs," she said with a grin. "You'd never know there were a hundred people here just a few nights ago."

"Shh," Jessica said, looking alarmed. She tiptoed over and shut the door. "Our parents still don't know about it."

"They don't?" Brooke asked. "A party that big is pretty hard to keep secret. I'm surprised the neighbors haven't told them—especially since the music was so loud."

"I know," Elizabeth said. "I've been worried about that."

The week before, Mr. and Mrs. Wakefield had taken a five-day trip to Mexico, leaving Elizabeth, Jessica, and their fourteen-year-old brother Steven in the care of May Brown, a baby-sitter who had seemed more like a tyrant. She made them eat things like broccoli casserole and go to bed at nine o'clock. On Saturday night, the twins and Steven had retaliated by tricking May out of the house and throwing a huge party, which ended in a food fight. Things were so bad that all three of them were actually glad when May came back and evicted the troublemakers. Cleanup had taken all Sunday morning, and Elizabeth still wasn't sure they hadn't missed something.

Jessica smiled at Elizabeth and tossed her long blond hair. "You're just a worrywart," she said. "There's not a single shred of evidence pointing to that party. They'll never find out, not in a million years."

Elizabeth grinned at her twin. "Well, I'm your big sister. I'm the one who's *supposed* to worry about things, remember?"

It was true that Elizabeth was the "older" of the twins. Even though Jessica and Elizabeth looked exactly alike, with their long blond hair, sparkling blue eyes, and dimples in their left cheeks, their personalities were as different as night and day. Elizabeth was four minutes older than Jessica and a lot more responsible. She spent her time working on *The Sweet Valley Sixers*, the sixth-grade newspaper, or reading Amanda Howard mysteries. Jessica liked to hang out at the Sweet Valley Mall with the Unicorns, the prettiest and most popular girls at Sweet Valley Middle School. They spent most of their time trying on clothes, planning sleepovers, and talking about boys and their favorite celebrities.

Jessica shrugged. "You can worry if you want to," she said. "I'm not going to worry until I *have* to."

"Well, I'm worried about my 'Meet the Stars' article," Brooke said. She turned to Elizabeth. "I was thinking of writing about Melody Power, but she hasn't come out with anything new in a while."

"I've got it!" Jessica said. "Shh. Listen!" She scrambled to her feet and turned up the volume on Elizabeth's radio. "Have you heard this yet? It's Coco! She's so amazing!"

For the next few minutes, the girls listened to Coco sing a mixture of English and French lyrics in a husky, breathless voice. "And there you have it, folks," the deejay said when the song ended. " 'Chocolate Kisses for My Baby,' sung especially for you by Coco, the hot new vocalist from France.

She's just releasing her first album in the U.S. This is definitely one to listen for."

Brooke had been listening intently to the song. "Wow, she is great. I wonder if she used to be in another band," she said. "There's something really familiar about her voice."

"She'd be perfect for your *Sixers* article!" Jessica said excitedly.

"It would be fun to do one of the articles on somebody really new," Elizabeth said.

Brooke nodded. "It might be a challenge, though," she said. "I wonder if anyone knows anything about her yet. I haven't read anything. Have you?"

Jessica shook her head. "Nope," she said. "I haven't even seen a picture of her. But that just makes her more exciting. She's a mystery."

"Maybe I could find out the label she records on and call the record company," Brooke said. "They could probably tell me something about her." She glanced at her watch and stood up. "Thanks a lot, you guys. I'd better go now. My mom is supposed to call tonight."

"Hey, that's right!" Elizabeth said. "Your mom's coming from Paris this week!" Brooke's parents were divorced, and when she had first moved to Sweet Valley everyone had thought she was really stuck-up. Elizabeth had felt terrible when she found out that Brooke wasn't stuck-up at all, but just upset about the divorce and sad that her mother had moved so far away.

"I can't wait," Brooke said with a grin. "Mom says she has a big surprise for me and I'm going crazy trying to figure out what it is!"

"What are you looking for?" Elizabeth asked as she and Jessica went into the kitchen for a snack. Steven was poking his head in the refrigerator, while a huge sandwich, an enormous glass of milk, and a plate of cookies sat waiting for him at the table.

"The pickles," Steven muttered. "We had a big jar of them. I won't enjoy my sandwich without a pickle."

"Give me a break, Steven," Jessica said. "You'd enjoy that sandwich if I stepped on it. Anyway, I'm sure they're in there somewhere." She dug into the cookie jar.

Elizabeth frowned. "Wait a minute. I think I remember seeing a guy wandering around with a jar of pickles on Saturday night."

Jessica snapped her fingers. "That's right,"

she said. "I spotted him raiding the refrigerator. I tried to get him to stop but he wouldn't."

"I wonder where he left the empty jar?" Elizabeth said.

"That reminds me," Steven said. "Look what I found in the upstairs laundry hamper." He pointed to an empty potato-chip bag sticking out of the garbage.

"Uh-oh," Elizabeth said. "I guess we missed it when we did the cleanup."

"Just hope we didn't miss anything else," Steven said grimly. "It'd be a real drag if Mom and Dad started asking questions about what went on here Saturday night."

"Listen, you guys," Jessica said confidently as she bit into another cookie. "Mom and Dad aren't going to suspect anything. We got everything cleaned up. And May didn't tell, so we're home free."

"What about the neighbors?" Elizabeth reminded her. "The music was so loud, I'm sure it could be heard all the way to the end of the block."

"We're lucky our next-door neighbors weren't home," Steven said. "They might have called the police."

Elizabeth nodded. "I'm worried about the Pearces. They live only two doors down, and Mrs. Pearce is as big a gossip as Caroline."

"There you go again, Worrywart," Jessica said with a grin.

"Maybe she's got something to worry about," Steven said. "Mrs. Pearce could give the whole thing away with one stupid remark."

"Maybe so," Jessica said, "but she and Mom don't see much of each other. The chances of her saying anything are pretty slim, if you ask me."

A few minutes later Mrs. Wakefield came in carrying a bag of groceries. "Hi, kids," she said cheerfully.

"Did you get some more cookies?" Jessica asked immediately.

Mrs. Wakefield laughed. "Yes, I did," she said. "You're still suffering from cookie withdrawal from when May was here, huh?"

"Yeah," Steven said. "But besides all the vegetables she made us eat, May turned out to be OK."

Mrs. Wakefield started putting groceries away. "I don't suppose it hurt you to go without junk food for five days," she said. "She must have fed you plenty of sandwiches, though."

Jessica laughed. "Are you kidding? Sandwiches taste good. She wouldn't let us get near a sandwich."

Mrs. Wakefield frowned. "If you didn't have sandwiches, what happened to all the mayonnaise?" she asked. "When we left, there was a jar in the refrigerator and another in the cupboard. They're both gone."

Elizabeth could feel herself blushing. They had used up the mayonnaise on the sandwiches for the party. "We, uh, didn't have sandwiches," she said, thinking quickly, "but we ate lots of salads."

"Right," Steven chimed in. "We had tons of salad. We ate so many salads I feel like a rabbit."

"And May ate lots of salad, too," Jessica said. "Every time I came into the kitchen, she was sitting at the table, eating a huge salad. With tons of mayonnaise," she added quickly.

"Well, I don't suppose an extra jar or two of mayonnaise matters," Mrs. Wakefield said. "Oh, by the way, I ran into Caroline Pearce's mother at the supermarket."

Elizabeth swallowed. "You . . . did?"

Mrs. Wakefield got out some potatoes to peel for dinner. "She was really impressed with the garage sale you kids put on last week."

"Really?" Jessica said.

"Yep. She thought it might be a good idea to have a neighborhood garage sale in a couple of weeks. She and I are going to organize it."

"You are? . . . Together?" Steven asked, shooting a worried glance at Elizabeth.

Mrs. Wakefield nodded. "These next few weeks are really going to be busy. One of your favorite people is coming to visit, too."

"Yeah?" Steven asked. "Who?"

"Your great-aunt Helen," Mrs. Wakefield replied.

"Aunt Helen!" Jessica exclaimed. "Hey, that's terrific! Last time she came, she brought those pretty silver bracelets for Elizabeth and me and a jazz trombone tape for Steven."

"I wonder what she'll bring us this time?" Steven said thoughtfully. "Maybe I could give her a few suggestions.

"Steven," Mrs. Wakefield scolded, "Aunt Helen isn't coming just to bring you presents."

"Just teasing," Steven said hastily. "Maybe

she'll get here in time for my band concert next week. Don't forget I'm doing a solo."

"I haven't forgotten," Mrs. Wakefield said. "Your father and I are planning to be there, but I'm afraid Aunt Helen won't be here yet. She's not coming until the following week. But she said to tell you all that she can't wait to see you."

"I can't wait, either," Elizabeth said.

At that moment, Mr. Wakefield came through the kitchen door. "Hi, everyone," he said. "You know, there must be ninety-eight empty potato-chip bags in the garbage cans in the garage."

Elizabeth, Steven, and Jessica looked at each other. *How are we going to explain this one?* Elizabeth wondered.

On Tuesday after school, Elizabeth went over to Brooke's house to spend the afternoon and have dinner. Brooke lived with her father in a pretty house that Mrs. Wakefield had decorated.

Elizabeth and Brooke were in the kitchen making spaghetti when the telephone rang in the den.

"I'll be right back," Brooke said. "There's a jar of spaghetti sauce in the cupboard. Would you open it while I get the phone?"

Elizabeth was stirring the sauce on the stove when Brooke came back into the kitchen a few minutes later, her brown eyes shining.

"That was my mom," Brooke announced happily. "She's getting in on Friday afternoon, and she wants me to come to her hotel after school."

Elizabeth smiled. "That's great, Brooke. You must be so excited to see her."

Brooke nodded. "I can't wait to see my baby sister, too," she said. "Sonya's over a year old and I've never met her. And I'll be glad to see my stepdad, Bobby, again. He's a free-lance writer, and he's very cool."

"How long have they lived in France?" Elizabeth asked.

"A couple of years." Suddenly Brooke's face grew dark and her brown eyes clouded. "I wanted them to stay here, so we could all be together. But when they decided to move to France, the judge said I couldn't go. I had to stay in California where I could be with my dad."

"That must really have been tough," Elizabeth said sympathetically.

"It is tough," Brooke said unhappily. "I love my father, and I know he works hard to make a nice home for us. But I've never stopped missing my mom. The first year was the worst, especially because she didn't call very often. I guess she needed to get used to her new life. After that, I got used to talking to her once a week on the phone. She writes once a week, too, and sends me presents. And I got to visit her and Bobby in Paris one time, too. I had fun, but it wasn't enough."

Elizabeth sat down on a kitchen stool. "I'm sure your mom wishes you could be together," she said. "It must be hard for her, too."

Brooke frowned. "Probably," she said. "But if she misses me as much as I miss her, why doesn't she move back to the United States so we could be together? I've never really understood why she had to go all the way to Paris in the first place. Talking on the phone and writing letters is OK. The presents are pretty nice, too, and I loved going to Paris. But a long-distance mom doesn't substitute for the real thing. I would give anything to have her move back."

Two

◇

"I wanted to tell you the latest about my research for my *Sixers* article," Brooke whispered to Elizabeth in the library Wednesday afternoon.

"I was wondering how it was going," Elizabeth whispered back. "I was just starting on mine."

"I was beginning to get worried because I read four different fan magazines and couldn't find anything about Coco," Brooke explained. "But then I called OmniArtists in Los Angeles—that's the company that released 'Chocolate Kisses' and 'Hot Coco.' The person I talked to gave me the name of Coco's agent." She looked down at a scrap of paper in her hand. "Her name is Ms. Martin. She has an office in Los Angeles. I called today at lunch, but her secretary said she's in New York and won't be back until tomorrow. She said that Ms. Martin will be glad to help me, though."

"That's great," Elizabeth said. "Maybe *The Sixers* will scoop the fan magazines."

"And guess what else," Brooke said. "The woman I talked to at OmniArtists promised to send me a photo. I can't wait to see what Coco looks like!"

While Elizabeth and Brooke walked out the library door Elizabeth's boyfriend, Todd Wilkins, and his friend Colin Harmon caught up with them.

"Hi, Elizabeth," Todd said. "I just overheard a couple of people talking about your party Saturday night. They said it was the greatest party they've ever been to." He grinned. "How does it feel to be famous?"

Elizabeth laughed. "I don't think I want to be famous for giving parties like that," she said.

"It was a lot of fun," Colin said. "Until the food fight, anyway. After that, things got a little crazy."

"A *little*?" Elizabeth asked. "You should have been around for the cleanup."

Colin laughed and looked over at Brooke. "Hey, Brooke, Amy Sutton told me you're writing an article on Coco for *The Sixers*."

Brooke nodded shyly. To Elizabeth's surprise, Brooke was blushing.

"I think she's great," Colin said. "I taped 'Hot Coco' off the radio so I can learn to play it on my guitar. I tried to get the album, but it hasn't even come out yet."

"Actually I talked to a woman at Coco's record company today, and she said Coco's first music video will be out on Monday."

"Fantastic!" Colin exclaimed. "Uh-oh, the bell's about to ring for math. I'll see you guys later."

Brooke smiled as Colin and Todd walked away. "Do you think Colin is cute?" she asked Elizabeth as the girls hurried to their next class.

"Uh-huh," Elizabeth said, watching her friend closely. "Do you?"

For a minute, Brooke didn't say anything. Then she smiled. "Maybe a little."

"Did you hear that Coco's first music video is coming out on Monday?" Lila Fowler asked Ellen

Riteman and Jessica as they were walking home from school together Wednesday afternoon.

"I can't wait to see her," Jessica said with a sigh. "It's kind of weird that nobody knows anything about her."

"Everybody was talking about Coco today," Ellen said. "She's got tons of fans in Sweet Valley, and she hasn't even put an album out yet."

"She *does* have a lot of fans in Sweet Valley," Jessica said thoughtfully. "Everywhere I went today, all I heard was *Coco Coco Coco*. There must be enough Coco crazies at Sweet Valley Middle School to start a fan club."

"A fan club!" Lila exclaimed. "Jessica what a *terrific* idea! A Coco fan club, right here in Sweet Valley!"

"Yeah!" Ellen said excitedly. "We should organize it. I'm sure all the Unicorns would join."

"That *would* be fun," Jessica agreed. "But I'm not sure how you do it. Mary Wallace's cousin in Chicago started a Johnny Buck fan club, and she told Mary that being president took up practically all her time."

"I'm sure you can handle it, Jessica," Lila said confidently. "Why don't you call Coco's record company and ask them how to start it. Of course," she added generously, "*you* get to be president."

"You'll make a super president, Jess," Ellen said with a big smile.

Jessica frowned. She had the feeling Lila and Ellen wanted her to be president because they didn't want to have to do all the work. But the idea of the fan club *was* exciting, and the more she thought about it, the better the word "president" sounded.

A few minutes later, Jessica walked into her house and called OmniArtists record company, while Lila and Ellen stood close-by.

"Hi, my name is Jessica Wakefield," she said. "My friends and I are big fans of Coco's, and we'd like to start a fan club in Sweet Valley. Can you give us some information on how to organize it?"

"Hello, Jessica," the woman said enthusiastically, "and congratulations!"

"Congratulations?" Jessica asked. "What for?"

"For being the first to volunteer! Your fan club will be Coco's first in the United States."

"Wow!" Jessica exclaimed.

"That's terrific!" Lila whispered.

"I bet we'll get lots of publicity," Ellen added.

"Have you thought of a name yet?" the woman asked.

Jessica hadn't, but all of a sudden a name popped into her head. "We'll call it Coco Crazy," she replied.

"Wonderful. I'll send you a packet of material that has some organizational tips and ideas for getting started."

"That would be great," Jessica said. "Will there be some stuff about Coco in the packet? A picture, maybe? Or some information about her?"

"I'm sure I can send you a picture. Her album won't be out for another couple of weeks, but her first video will be released on Monday. Coco will be coming to L.A. from Paris to do some promotion this week, so you can look for her on local TV."

"That's fantastic!" Jessica exclaimed.

"In the meantime, I'll call several of the fan magazines and let them know that you're starting the first fan club. They'll probably get in touch with you about some publicity."

"Terrific," Jessica said happily.

"Wow," Lila whispered.

Jessica gave the woman her address and said good-bye.

"This is great!" Jessica yelled. "We're going to be famous!"

"When will we have our first meeting?" Ellen asked eagerly.

"As soon as I get the stuff from OmniArtists," Jessica promised.

"We'll have to call a special meeting to tell the Unicorns about it," Ellen said.

Jessica smiled. "Can you believe it?" she said to Lila. "We're the very first Coco fan club in the country!"

Lila didn't look quite so happy. "Are you sure you want to be president, Jess? It *is* a lot of work."

"Jessica and Steven," Mrs. Wakefield said, coming into the den where they were watching TV. "I was wondering if either of you could tell me anything about the slice of bologna I found in my closet."

Jessica and Steven exchanged horrified glances. "Bologna in your closet?" Jessica asked.

"I have to admit that I was a little surprised," Mrs. Wakefield said. "It was in my shoe."

"Well, gosh, I don't know . . ." Steven began.

"It was May," Jessica said firmly. "May did it."

Mrs. Wakefield raised her eyebrows. "May?"

"Yes," Jessica lied. "You see, May wouldn't let *us* eat sandwiches, but she ate them all the time. In secret."

"Jessica's right," Steven said. "I guess she was ashamed. I mean, after she made this big deal about eating vegetables and everything, she probably didn't want us to see *her* eating sandwiches. So she sneaked away to do it."

"To my *closet*?" Mrs. Wakefield asked, raising her eyebrows.

"I know it sounds weird," Jessica said, "but May was pretty weird. Nice but weird."

Mrs. Wakefield frowned. "I'm worried," she said thoughtfully, "that there's something that you children aren't telling me about what went on while we were gone."

"Oh, *no*, Mom," Jessica and Steven said in unison. Hurriedly, Jessica added, "Listen, Mom, I was just on my way to the kitchen to set the table."

Steven swung his feet off the sofa. "And I was on my way to the garage to get out the mower. I know Dad wants me to mow the front yard."

Mrs. Wakefield shook her head. "You're going to set the table and you're going to mow the lawn?" She smiled at them suspiciously. "Now I *know* something is wrong."

On Thursday afternoon, Jessica hurried home from school and shrieked with excitement when she saw a package on the hallway table with TO MISS JESSICA WAKEFIELD, PRESIDENT, COCO CRAZY FAN CLUB written on it. She was pulling it open at the kitchen table when Elizabeth appeared at the door.

"Hi, Jess," Elizabeth said cheerfully. "What's that?"

"The stuff from OmniArtists for my fan club," Jessica said happily. She pulled out an 8" x 10" color photo. "Look, Liz! They sent a photo of Coco—autographed! Wow, she's beautiful."

Elizabeth dropped her books on the counter and came over to look. The woman in the color photograph had large brown eyes and long brown hair that was swept back on the sides and fell in long curls over her shoulders. She was dressed in faded jeans, a fringed suede jacket, and red cowboy boots. Across the bottom of the photo was written, "To Jessica, My Number One Fan, Love Coco."

"She's really pretty," Elizabeth agreed. "Somehow she looks the way she sounds."

"Just wait until Lila and Ellen see *this*," Jessica said. "They'll absolutely *die* with envy. I'll bet nobody else in the entire United States has an autographed picture of Coco!"

"What's this other stuff?" Elizabeth asked, poking through the contents of the box.

"I don't know. Just stuff about how to start the fan club. Hey, I've got a pair of cowboy boots in my closet upstairs—maybe I could color them with red shoe polish."

"You could try," Elizabeth said.

"You know what, Elizabeth, Coco looks really familiar. There's something about her eyes—"

"Hey! T-shirts!" Elizabeth said, pulling them out of the package. "Six of them." She unfolded one and held it up. It was white with COCO CRAZY! printed in red letters inside a big red heart.

"It's *beautiful*!" Jessica said. "I can't wait to try it on!" She snatched it and dashed up the stairs to her room.

"But what about this other stuff?" Elizabeth

called up the stairs after her. "Don't you want to find out how to start your fan club?"

"The fan club can wait," Jessica cried. "I have to show Lila and Ellen our new T-shirts!" A minute later, she ran down the stairs, wearing her new T-shirt and carrying her backpack. She grabbed two more of the shirts and the autographed picture and stuffed them into her backpack.

"Do I get one?" Elizabeth asked. "And how about Brooke? We're fans, too."

"Sure," Jessica said impatiently, and headed out the door. Coco Crazy was about to hold its first unofficial meeting!

"I couldn't reach Coco's agent," Brooke said, as she followed Elizabeth into the kitchen later that afternoon. "She's back from France, and Coco's with her. But the two of them were doing promotions in New York today. They won't be in L.A. until tomorrow."

"Maybe you can catch her then," Elizabeth said.

"I hope," Brooke replied. She looked at the papers on the kitchen table. "What's all this stuff?"

"It's the stuff that the record company sent to help Jessica start her fan club," Elizabeth said.

"That's great," Brooke said.

"And here's your very own Coco T-shirt," Elizabeth said, taking one out of the package. "Will this fit?"

"It looks perfect," Brooke said. She sat down at the kitchen table.

"There was an autographed picture of Coco in the package, too, but Jessica took it over to Lila's." Elizabeth opened the refrigerator. "I'm having a sandwich," she said. "Do you want one?"

"Sure. Elizabeth," Brooke said tentatively, "what was it like when you first . . . uh, when you first thought you liked Todd?"

Elizabeth put the sandwich in front of Brooke and sat down across from her. "Everything was kind of mixed up. I knew I liked him, but I wasn't sure he liked me, except as a friend. In fact, for a while I thought he liked Jessica *instead* of me, and I was convinced I'd really messed things up between us. It wasn't until the bowling party that we realized that we liked each other." She picked up her sandwich and smiled at Brooke. "I bet I know why you're asking," she added.

Brooke blushed. "I guess it's pretty obvious," she said. "Colin has been really friendly lately—like when we saw him and Todd yesterday." She took a bite out of her sandwich.

"I got that feeling, too." Elizabeth smiled. "Maybe you and Colin and Todd and I can all go biking together this weekend."

"I'd love to," Brooke said. "But I can't this weekend."

"That's right!" Elizabeth said. "Your mom will be here."

Brooke looked down.

"What's wrong?" Elizabeth asked, surprised. "I thought you were looking forward to it."

"I am," Brooke said. "I mean, I really want to see her—it's been such a long time, and I've missed her so much." She bit her lip. "But I'm scared, too."

"She's your *mom*," Elizabeth said. "What's there to be scared about?"

"I know it's hard to understand if you have a mom around all the time," Brooke said thoughtfully. "But I haven't seen mine in months. I've changed a lot since then—what if she's changed, too? What if she doesn't feel like my mother anymore? And there's Sonya, too, and Bobby."

"You like your stepfather, don't you?" Elizabeth asked.

"Sure," Brooke replied. "He's really neat. But he and Mom have a new baby. I'm not jealous— at least I don't think I am. But they're a family, and I don't feel like I'm part of it."

"But you *are* part of it," Elizabeth said, leaning forward. "Your mom must want you to be in the family, Brooke, or she wouldn't come all the way from Europe just to see you."

Brooke frowned. "Yeah, but maybe they didn't come to see me," she said. "Maybe they're here on business or something. I don't know what's going on and that's what scares me. Maybe seeing me is just an afterthought, or something they thought they had to do."

"You know what I think?" Elizabeth said. "I think your mom loves you a lot and is probably really excited to see you tomorrow."

Brooke gave Elizabeth a small smile. "I hope you're right. Maybe I should concentrate on how I wish things would turn out, rather than what I'm scared of."

Elizabeth nodded. "If you had a wish, what would it be?"

Brooke didn't hesitate. "I wish Mom and

Bobby would move back to California—to Sweet Valley. I'd probably still live with my dad, but at least we could be together. I'd get to see my little sister grow up, and I'd get to see Mom whenever I wanted. That's my all-time dream.''

Three

◇

"Hi, Brooke."

Brooke looked up, surprised. Colin Harmon fell into step beside her as she left school on Friday. Suddenly her cheeks felt warm. "Hi," she said.

He glanced down at the small suitcase she was carrying. "Are you going away for the weekend?"

"Yes, but not far," Brooke said. "My mom and stepdad and baby sister are in Sweet Valley for a visit. I'm taking the bus to the Sweet Valley Plaza to spend the weekend with them."

"The bus stop's on my way," Colin said. "I'll walk with you."

Brooke nodded, wishing she could think of something to say. Usually she didn't have trouble talking to boys, but Colin made her feel shy.

"It's great that you get to be with your mom," Colin said thoughtfully. "I wish I could spend the weekend with my dad, but he lives in New York."

"I guess you don't get to see him very often," Brooke said.

"Summers, mostly," Colin replied in a matter-of-fact tone. "And once in a while he comes here to see me. But he's pretty busy. He's got a new family."

"So does my mom," Brooke said. "She's married again, and I've got a new little sister." She couldn't keep the unhappiness out of her voice, and Colin gave her a quick, sympathetic look.

"It's hard to get used to it at first," he said. "I'll bet you're nervous. I always am when I'm going to see my dad."

"Yeah, I guess I am," Brooke admitted. "I haven't seen my mom for a long time. I've been wondering if she's changed and whether she'll be so busy with my little sister that she won't have time for me." She was glad that they'd reached the bus stop, because she had the uncomfortable feeling that she'd said too much. She didn't usually share her feelings with people, except for her close friends. But something about Colin made her open up.

"I know how you feel," Colin said. He glanced at the T-shirt she was wearing. "Hey, I like your T-shirt. How's your article coming?"

"I called Coco's agent twice today," Brooke said, "but she wasn't there."

"I'm sure you'll find her. Well, have a great weekend with your mom," Colin said. He smiled and walked off.

Brooke stared after him. It was nice to know that she and Colin had something in common.

When the big green bus pulled up, Brooke took the seat behind the driver and put her suitcase on the empty seat next to her. As she looked out the window, she thought of her mother and the last time they'd been together in Paris. They'd had a lot of fun, shopping and sight-seeing together, eating with Bobby in funny little cafés along the River Seine. *But that was before Sonya was born*, Brooke reminded herself uneasily. *What will it be like now that they're a family?*

Fifteen minutes later, the bus stopped a block from the Sweet Valley Plaza. Brooke got out and walked to the hotel, feeling more nervous by the minute. "I'd like the room number for Mrs. Constance Gray," she told the clerk at the registration desk.

"She's in Suite 505," the clerk said, smiling. "Just take the elevator in the corner."

The elevator ride seemed to take forever. Brooke could see herself reflected in the mirrors that lined the elevator—a slender girl with wavy brown hair, large brown eyes, wearing jeans, sneakers, and a COCO CRAZY! T-shirt. She got out at the fifth floor and walked slowly down the hall to Suite 505. She'd barely knocked once when the door swung open, and she was soon hugging her mother.

"Brooke!" Mrs. Gray cried tearfully. "Brooke, I'm so glad to see you!"

"Me, too," Brooke whispered, burying her face against her mother's shoulder and hugging her back. For a long while they held each other.

"Now," Mrs. Gray said, holding Brooke at arm's length, "let me see you." She pulled in her breath. "You're so much taller—and beautiful! I can't believe how much older you look!" Suddenly she looked surprised. "And what's this T-shirt you're wearing?"

"Oh, Coco's a terrific new rock star. Everybody at school loves her. We started a fan club called Coco Crazy." She looked at her mother, who was wearing black leggings and a blue sweatshirt. "You've changed, too, Mom. You're thinner. And you've let your hair grow." Mrs. Gray's brown hair fell below her shoulders in pretty waves.

Mrs. Gray laughed and tossed her head. "I'm thinner, because I've been working out every day since Sonya was born. And I changed my hair style because—" She smiled. "But that can wait until later. Bobby's playing tennis, but he told me to tell you he'll be back as soon as he can. He's anxious to see you." She paused, listening. "I think somebody else is anxious to see you, too."

At that moment, Brooke heard a small, sleepy cry. "Sonya!" she exclaimed.

"Come and meet your little sister," Mrs. Gray said happily. She opened the bedroom door and Brooke followed her into the room. There, standing in a crib, was a chubby little girl wearing a pink cotton nightgown with a white ruffle around the bottom. Her big brown eyes looked sleepy, and when she opened her mouth to yawn Brooke could see two tiny white teeth.

"She's so sweet!" Brooke whispered. "Can I pick her up?"

"Of course," her mother said, smiling. So for the next ten minutes, Brooke held her little sister and tickled her toes to make her laugh. Then she and her mother changed Sonya's wet diaper, dressed her in a yellow jumpsuit and tiny yellow sneakers, and took her into the living room where they all sat on the sofa together.

Mrs. Gray looked from Brooke to Sonya. "You know," she said thoughtfully, "Sonya looks just the way you did at her age."

Brooke giggled as Sonya tugged at her hair. "I was chubby?"

"You were *adorable*," her mother replied, "and I can't get over how beautiful you are, now that you're so grown up. I almost forgot," she said as she stood up. "Bobby and I brought you some presents."

"Presents?" Brooke said. "Just having you and Sonya and Bobby here is enough." But after she sniffed the French perfume, modeled the jewelry, and tried on the jacket her mother and stepdad had brought her, Brooke had to admit that the presents were pretty nice, too.

"I have two other surprises for you," Mrs.

Gray said, sitting down opposite Brooke. "Are you ready?"

"More surprises?" Brooke asked eagerly. "Sure, I'm ready!"

Mrs. Gray sat back in her chair. "The first is that Bobby and I have decided to move back to California," she said. "We're looking at houses already, here in Sweet Valley and in Los Angeles. Until we find something, we'll stay here at the hotel so we can be near you. We want you to stay with us whenever you can."

Brooke could only stare at her mom, speechless. Her dream was coming true! They would all be together!

Mrs. Gray was watching her closely. "Well, how does that sound?"

"I . . . I . . ." Brooke stammered. "Oh, Mom, it's wonderful! It's what I've been hoping for!"

"Oh, good! It's been a long time, and you're growing up so fast. I was afraid you might be so busy with your friends that you wouldn't . . . well, that you wouldn't have time for us."

Brooke grinned. So her mother had been worried just the way she had! "This is the best surprise I can think of," she said. "Now what's the second surprise?"

Mrs. Gray stood up. "The other surprise is about me," she said. "I have a new career now."

"A new career?" Brooke asked. She remembered that her mother had done some acting when they lived in Hollywood. "What is it?"

"Remember when I was taking voice lessons?" her mother asked. "My voice coach thought I was good enough to sing professionally," Mrs. Gray went on. "After Bobby and I were married, I found an agent who promised to help me get started—but only if we would move to Europe. She thought it would be easier for me to get a start there, because there's less competition and American singers are in such demand there. She was right, too. I've done very well."

"So *that's* why you moved!" Brooke exclaimed. "I thought you just wanted to live in Europe."

"It wasn't that we *wanted* to live there," her mother replied. "After all, it meant leaving you here, and I hated that. I thought it would be only for a year or so, but I had to stop working for a while when I had Sonya. So it took longer than we expected to make a successful start."

Brooke felt so happy that she thought she would burst. Her mother *hadn't* wanted to move to Europe without her! "Are you successful now?" she asked.

Mrs. Gray nodded, grinning slightly. "It's actually hard for me to believe how well things are going. My singles are popular, and my debut album is selling amazingly well. Both are being released here in the States this week, and Bernice, my agent, is setting up my first American appearances."

"That's terrific, Mom," Brooke said proudly, trying to imagine her mother onstage as a professional singer. "Does that mean you're going to be famous?"

Mrs. Gray smiled and stood up. "Would you like to hear my most popular single?"

"Yeah," Brooke replied, sitting on the edge of the sofa. She'd heard her mom sing before, of course, but that had been a long time ago, when she was little and the songs had been mostly lullabies. She had no idea what kind of songs her mother sang now. Golden oldies? Folk music? Jazz? Rhythm and blues?

Mrs. Gray went to the stereo and put on a tape. Then she turned and watched Brooke. "I'm excited to see your reaction," she said.

Brooke leaned forward to catch the first notes. But what she heard was so incredible that for a moment she couldn't believe it.

What she heard was the throaty, sexy sound of Coco singing "Chocolate Kisses for My Baby"!

"Mom?" she whispered incredulously. "Are you sure you put on the right tape?"

"That's me, honey," her mom said.

"That's *you*? I don't believe it!" Brooke exclaimed. "You're *Coco*!"

Mrs. Gray wrapped her arms around Brooke. "Are you surprised?"

"*Surprised!*" "I'm . . . I'm . . ." Brooke couldn't think of a word to describe how she felt.

"You're speechless," Mrs. Gray said, laughing. "Wait a sec," she said, fumbling through a bag. She handed Brooke a framed, autographed photo that said "To my beautiful daughter, from her loving mother, Coco!" The picture showed a beautiful woman with brown eyes and long brown hair, dressed in faded jeans, a fringed suede jacket, and red cowboy boots.

"Oh, wow," Brooke said, looking at the photo. And then she laughed. Imagine what her mother must have thought when she came in wearing her Coco Crazy T-shirt! "I can't wait to tell the kids at school," she said. "Isn't it funny? I'm supposed to be writing an article about you for *The Sixers*, our class newspaper! And my friend Jessica is president of your fan club. Isn't that amazing? They're going to go bananas when they hear that you're my mom!"

As she looked at the photo, Brooke imagined Coco onstage, surrounded by millions of adoring fans. She imagined Coco pulling her onstage and introducing her to all her fans, while people cheered and flashbulbs popped! She was Coco's daughter! *Wow!*

Brooke's fantasy was interrupted by an authoritative knock at the door. Mrs. Gray started toward it, but it opened before she reached it and a woman came in. She was tall and thin, with dark hair pulled back into a bun and piercing dark eyes behind gold-rimmed glasses. She wore a tailored gray business suit.

"Well, Constance," the woman said briskly. "Have you told her yet?"

Mrs. Gray frowned. "I'd like to give this a little more thought, Bernice. I'm not sure that—"

"Then I'll tell her myself," the woman interrupted. She turned to Brooke, holding out her hand. "I am your mother's agent, Bernice Martin."

"You're the woman I tried to call!" Brooke exclaimed, shaking the woman's hand. She laughed. "You see, I was trying to get an interview with Coco for my school paper, and I hoped that you could—"

Bernice put an arm around Brooke's shoulders and led her to the sofa. "Brooke, dear," she said, patting the seat next to her, "we have some *very* important things to talk about."

Brooke laughed. "I guess I don't have to worry about getting an interview now, do I?"

"I wasn't talking about the interview," Bernice said, trying to cover up her impatience. "I was talking about your mother's career. You know how important it is to her, don't you?"

"I guess," Brooke said, beginning to feel uncomfortable.

"And you want to help her succeed, don't you?" Bernice asked.

"Sure I do," Brooke said. She looked across the room at her mother and smiled. "Why?"

"You have a very important role in your mother's career," Bernice said smoothly. She smiled a thin, tight-lipped smile that showed perfect white teeth. "You see, Brooke, as far as other people are concerned, you have to pretend that you don't exist."

"Bernice—" Mrs. Gray began.

"Don't exist?" Brooke asked. "What do you mean?"

Bernice laughed. "Let me explain it in very simple terms. In the rock music business, it's not absolutely crucial to have a good voice. What you *have* to have, above everything else, is an image. Your mother and I have gone to a great deal of work to develop Coco's image, and so far we've been very successful. Unfortunately, that image doesn't include a husband, a baby, and especially not a twelve-year-old daughter. In France, we managed to keep Bobby and Sonya under wraps. We did that by developing an aura of mystery around your mother. Now, we need to keep *you* under wraps as well."

Brooke looked worriedly at her mother. "But what am I supposed to do?" she asked. "Am I supposed to disappear or something?"

Mrs. Gray bit her lip. "Bernice," she said, "perhaps we'd better reconsider this whole—"

Bernice smiled again at Brooke. "I see that I

haven't explained things very well," she said. "Let me ask you this, Brooke. How would you feel if you opened a fan magazine and read that Johnny Buck was married and had a twelve-year-old daughter?"

Brooke frowned. "Well, I—" she began, but Bernice didn't let her finish.

"I'll tell you how you'd feel," she said. "You'd feel *bored*. Married rock stars, especially married rock stars with children, are absolutely *boring*. And the sad truth is that rock stars who are boring stop being rock stars. Fans are young, and they like stars close to their own age. If Coco's fans find out she has a twelve-year-old daughter, they'll know that she's much older than she looks. If Coco's image is ruined she can kiss her hard-earned career good-bye. Is *that* what you want?"

Brooke looked at her mother. "No, I guess not," she mumbled.

"Did you hear that, Constance?" Bernice said triumphantly. "Your daughter wants you to be a success just like the rest of us." She looked back at Brooke. "Which means, of course, that you can't tell *anyone* that you are Coco's daughter."

"Mom!" Brooke exclaimed. "That means I have to *lie!*"

"No, it doesn't," Bernice said. "It just means that you have to keep quiet."

Mrs. Gray sighed. "I know you don't like this, Brooke, and neither do I. But it worked in France. Let's see if we can make it work here—at least for a little while. OK?"

Bernice leaned forward so that her face was only a few inches from Brooke's. "I want you to promise me," she said, very seriously, "that you will not tell *anyone* who your mother is."

"Not anyone?" Brooke asked. "Not even my father?"

"Your father will probably have to know at some point," Bernice said. "But not now. For now, this has to be our little secret. Promise?"

Brooke hesitated. "I . . . promise," she said finally. But the words hurt. She felt like she hadn't fit into her mother's life for a long time, and now, just when she thought they had a chance to be like a normal mother and daughter again—*this*. It didn't seem fair.

Brooke looked at her mother. She knew there was a lot to be excited about this afternoon— seeing her mother again, meeting Sonya, and especially finding out that her mother was moving back to California. But instead she felt scared.

Scared that there would never be room for her in her mother's life.

"Brooke, you're so grown up!" Bobby exclaimed when he came in from the tennis court a few minutes later. "And you look more like your mom every day."

"I've told Brooke the rules of our little game, Bobby," Bernice said. "She's agreed to abide by them." She glanced at her watch. "Now, if you'll excuse me, I have an appointment. I'll talk to you tomorrow, Coco."

When Bernice was gone, Bobby turned to Brooke, his face suddenly serious. "I know this scheme of Bernice's sounds crazy," he said. "And I have to say that I don't like it. But your mom's work is important to her, and Bernice has been right about everything else so far." He grinned at her mother. "I'm going along with it, at least for now."

Brooke relaxed a little. Bobby was still the warm, affectionate person she remembered. At least not *everything* had changed.

The rest of the evening was fun. They ordered room service for dinner, and Brooke chose a triple-decker hamburger with bacon and cheese. They played with Sonya until her bedtime and then Brooke told her mother and Bobby all about school and her friends and her life in Sweet Valley.

They had strawberry pancakes and hot chocolate from room service the next morning, and then Mrs. Gray asked Brooke what she'd like to do that day.

"I'd like to go to the aquarium," Brooke said. "They've got some baby sea otters I'd love to see."

Mrs. Gray frowned. "I'm afraid that Bernice wants me to keep a low profile, Brooke. Maybe we'd better—"

At that moment, the phone rang. "Hello, Bernice," Mrs. Gray said. Then she frowned. "Los Angeles, in an hour? But Brooke and Bobby and Sonya and I were planning to—" She broke off, listening, then she sighed. "Well, I suppose," she said. When she hung up, she turned to Brooke.

"I'm sorry, honey, but something's come up. You and Bobby and Sonya will have to go to the aquarium without me."

"But I thought we were going to do something *together*!" Brooke protested.

"Bernice has managed to get me an interview with *Rolling Rocks Magazine*," Mrs. Gray said. "It's something I really should do, Brooke. Bernice thinks it's a great opportunity." She smiled. "I'll be back this evening, and we'll all have dinner together. In the meantime, you and Bobby and Sonya will have a great time at the aquarium."

Bobby put his hand on Brooke's shoulder. "Don't look so glum, honey," he said softly. "We'll have a lot of fun—just us and the sea otters."

So Brooke, Bobby, and Sonya spent Saturday watching baby sea otters and sharks at the aquarium. On Sunday, Brooke and Bobby played tennis and swam in the hotel pool while Coco, Bernice, and a couple of costume designers spent most of the day planning costumes for the performances Bernice was arranging in Las Vegas and Los Angeles.

By the time Brooke went home on Sunday night, she felt very close to her stepdad and her little sister. But somehow her mother still felt very far away.

When her father asked her on Sunday evening how her weekend with her mother had gone, she managed to smile and say, "I had a really great time."

But inside she knew she was lying. She felt sad and scared, and it was all because of her mom's new career.

Four

◇

"Did you have fun with your mom this weekend?" Elizabeth asked Brooke as they were getting their books out of their lockers on Monday morning.

"It was OK," Brooke said evasively. "Mom was pretty busy, though. I didn't get to see much of her."

"Really?" Elizabeth asked. "What was she doing?"

Brooke frowned. She couldn't tell the truth—she'd promised Bernice. But she hated to lie. The safest thing was just to say as little as possible. "Oh, just stuff," she said vaguely. "I had a good time with Bobby and Sonya, though. And they're moving back to California."

"They are!" Elizabeth exclaimed. "That's wonderful! Your wish is coming true!"

"Yeah." Brooke sighed, wishing she could tell Elizabeth how she was really feeling. But if she did, she would give away Coco's secret.

In English class Brooke noticed that Jessica, Lila, Ellen, and Mandy Miller were all wearing their Coco Crazy T-shirts, and she couldn't stop thinking about her mother. She was so distracted that Mr. Bowman had to call her name three times, loudly, to get her attention.

"What's the matter, Brooke?" he asked when she finally looked up. "Have you gone Coco crazy, too?" Everybody in English class giggled, and Brooke felt her cheeks flaming red. *If they only knew!* she thought.

It isn't fair, she told herself angrily, walking down the hall after English. *How can they expect me to keep all this a secret?* She was so deep in thought that she didn't see Jessica, Lila, Ellen, and Mandy coming toward her until she almost bumped into them.

"Hi, Brooke," Jessica said. She was wearing

faded jeans and red cowboy boots. "Hey, where's your Coco T-shirt?"

"Yeah," Lila added, "haven't you heard the new club rule?"

"What rule?" Brooke asked, looking from one to the other.

"All the charter members of Coco Crazy have to wear their T-shirts every day this week," Jessica explained. "We're advertising the club so we can recruit new members."

Mandy grinned. "We're having a lot of luck, too. *Everybody* wants to join!"

Brooke bit her lip. "I—I don't know," she stammered.

Ellen put her hands on her hips, frowning. "What's the matter, Brooke?" she asked. "Aren't you a charter member of the club?"

"I . . . I guess," Brooke mumbled. Her throat was beginning to feel dry, and she couldn't say any more. She was glad when the bell rang.

At lunch that Monday, Jessica and the Unicorns were gathered around their usual table, which they called the Unicorner.

"Listen, everybody," Lila said, rapping her

spoon loudly on the table to get their attention. "I want to announce that Coco Crazy is holding a party this afternoon at my house to celebrate Coco's new video being released on STV today. I want everybody to come. We have a giant-screen TV, you know, and my housekeeper promised to make lots of chocolate stuff in honor of Coco."

"Can I invite Aaron Dallas?" Jessica asked. Everyone knew that Jessica had a crush on Aaron.

"Sure," Lila said. "Let's invite lots of people."

"Aaron's a big Coco fan," Jessica explained. "And you know what? He promised to lend me his buckskin jacket. It's got fringe on it, just like Coco's!"

"Mmm," Lila said enviously. When she saw Elizabeth, Amy Sutton, and Brooke approaching, she waved them over to the table. "There's a fan club party at my house this afternoon," she said. "Everybody's invited to watch Coco's new music video and eat lots of chocolate."

"Great!" Amy said. " 'Chocolate Kisses' is the best song I've ever heard. Can I invite Ken Matthews too?"

"Sure," Lila said generously. "We need lots of members for the fan club. We're all going to sign a big banner telling Coco how much we love her!"

"Brooke, you're coming, right?" Jessica asked.

To Jessica's amazement, Brooke shook her head. "I don't think I can," she said slowly.

"Why not?" Jessica asked.

Brooke shrugged. "Uh . . . I've got other things to do." She fiddled with the hem of her shirt. "Anyway, I don't see why everybody's going so crazy over a singer. She's just a person, after all." She turned and walked away. Elizabeth and Amy traded puzzled looks, then walked after her.

"Well, if she's got other things to do," Ellen said, "she can do them—by herself."

"Quiet, everybody!" Lila yelled later that afternoon. "The video is starting!"

The room fell silent as Lila turned up the volume on the big-screen TV.

"And now, the moment you've all been waiting for. Here's Coco, the fabulous new star from Paris, with her debut music video—'Hot Coco'!"

The huge color screen was suddenly filled

with the image of a beautiful brown-haired, brown-eyed woman wearing faded jeans, a fringed jacket, and red cowboy boots. Behind her was a band made up of a drummer, a bass player, and a guitarist. She held the microphone and began to sing, dancing with fast, graceful movements across a dark set lit with shimmering neon lights.

"Wow, she can *sing*!" Aaron said.

"She's a terrific dancer, too," Mandy said, her eyes fixed on the screen.

"Fantastic," Jessica agreed, snuggling into the buckskin jacket Aaron had loaned her. She smiled proudly, feeling that she helped make Coco famous. After all, there wouldn't be a Coco Crazy fan club if *she* hadn't gotten the idea!

When the video was over, everybody clapped and whistled. "Guess what?" Lila said. "While the video was playing, I taped it on our VCR. Who wants to see it again?"

While Jessica and the other members of Coco Crazy were watching Coco's video at Lila's house, Brooke was also watching it—on the VCR in her bedroom. Before she had left the hotel on Sunday,

Bobby had handed her a shopping bag full of Coco tapes, posters, publicity shots, bumper stickers, more T-shirts, and the video.

I just don't believe it, Brooke thought as she watched her mother perform the dance routine that was part of "Hot Coco." *That's my mom up there, doing her thing in front of the whole, entire world—and I can't tell anybody who she is!*

Brooke sat up on her bed and pulled her knees up under her chin, wrapping her arms around her legs. It was hard enough that she had to keep her mother's life a secret. It didn't help that all her friends dressed like Coco, threw Coco parties, and talked about Coco constantly. She felt like she was suffocating. She hadn't meant to snap at Jessica that afternoon when she'd invited her to Lila's party. It was just hard to take. If she didn't watch out, she'd soon be back in the spot she was in when she came to Sweet Valley— alone, without any friends.

The video was over. Brooke put her forehead on her knees, feeling the tears come to her eyes. *And now I'm miserable again*, she thought, *but this time it's because Mom has come back. And I still don't fit into her life.*

* * *

Elizabeth, Todd, and Colin walked home together from the fan club video party. Todd had had basketball practice that afternoon, so he arrived at Lila's only a few minutes before the party was over—just in time to get a couple of pieces of fudge and a dish of chocolate ice cream.

"Sorry I was late," he said. "Did I miss much?"

"If you got to see the video and grab some of Lila's food, you didn't miss anything," Colin told him with a grin. Colin looked at Elizabeth. "Where was Brooke? She's such a Coco fan—I thought she'd be there."

"She was invited," Elizabeth said, "but she didn't want to come."

"Maybe she's with her mother," Colin said. "She's still in town, isn't she?"

"I guess so," Elizabeth said. "Brooke said they were going to be here for a few days." She frowned. In fact she had asked Brooke several times about her mother and what they had done over the weekend, but Brooke had barely replied. It was as if she were deliberately avoiding the subject.

"She's probably with her mom, then," Colin said. "When my dad comes for a visit, I want to spend every minute I can with him."

"Yeah, probably," Todd said, and Elizabeth agreed too. She knew that if she had been separated from *her* mother for a long time, she'd want to be with her every minute she could.

In her room, Brooke reached for the telephone and dialed her mother's hotel. The operator put her through, and in a minute the telephone in the Grays' suite was ringing. Brooke crossed her fingers. On the fourth ring, Bobby answered it.

"Hi, Brooke," he said cheerfully. "I was changing Sonya. What are you doing this afternoon? Want to come over and play some tennis before it gets dark?"

"Actually," Brooke broke in, "I was hoping I could talk to my mom. Is she around?"

Bobby hesitated. "No, I'm afraid she isn't," he said. "Today her music video was released. She and Bernice went to L.A. to do some promotion. Bernice got her a couple more big interviews."

"Oh," Brooke said. She uncrossed her fingers. Then she crossed them again. "What time will she be back?" she asked. "Maybe I could come and eat with you."

"Sonya and I would love to have you join us for dinner," Bobby said, "but your mom is staying in the city tonight. What about tomorrow? She's scheduled for a day off. She's been working pretty hard, and she needs to get some rest."

"A day off?" Brooke asked excitedly.

Bobby laughed. "Yeah. Isn't it great? A whole day with no interviews, no photos, no rehearsals. Would you like to come over after school? Maybe we could all do something together."

"That would be terrific," Brooke said. "Hey, I know what we could do! There's a place at the beach that has the most fantastic hot dogs anywhere. We could rent skateboards and—"

"Hey, slow down, sweetie," Bobby said with a laugh. "You're forgetting something."

"I am?" Brooke asked.

"Yeah. Bernice would rather we stay in the hotel, because she's afraid that somebody will recognize Coco and figure out our secret. How about if we rent some videos and watch old movies on TV? And maybe we can talk your mom into modeling some of her new costumes."

Brooke sighed. She wanted to spend time with her mom as a mom and not as a rock star, but seeing her in the hotel was better than not seeing her at all. "Tell Mom I'll be there right after school," she said.

"I know she'll be happy to hear that, Brooke," Bobby said. "She misses you every bit as much as you miss her—maybe more."

Brooke smiled. "Thanks, Bobby."

"Jessica," Mrs. Wakefield called that night. "Do you know where the dill pickles are? I'm sure there was a full jar in the refrigerator before we went to Mexico."

"Pickles?" she asked with an innocent look. "No, I don't know anything about pickles. But maybe you should ask May."

"Ask May? Why?"

"Because," Jessica said, thinking as fast as she could, "May really liked pickles. Especially dills. Every time I saw her she was eating a pickle." She widened her eyes. "You don't think she's going to have a baby, do you?"

Mrs. Wakefield laughed. "Don't be silly, Jessica. She probably just likes pickles. But an entire jar—" She shook her head. "First the mayonnaise, now the pickles. May is quite an eater, isn't she? And she's so thin, too.''

That night Jessica told Elizabeth about their mother's most recent discovery. "I know I said there was nothing to worry about," Jessica said, "but I have the terrible feeling that Mom and Dad are going to find out about the party."

Elizabeth nodded. "I keep waiting for the axe to fall."

"And Steven's worried, too," Jessica continued. "The other day he even volunteered to mow the grass to get Mom's mind off the bologna she found in her shoe."

"Maybe it would be better if we told them before they found out for themselves," Elizabeth said.

"Either way, I hate to think about it," Jessica said. "Anyway, we already learned our lesson: If you have a big party when your parents are out of town, keep the food *outside*."

Five

◇

"I bet you're going to see your mom," Colin said when he ran into Brooke at the bus stop the next day after school.

"Yep," Brooke said. "We're going to watch old movies, and Mom's going to show me some of her costumes."

"Costumes, huh," Colin asked. "Is she an actress?"

Brooke felt her insides tighten up. "Uh-huh," she said, and changed the subject as fast as she could. "I heard that you're getting a band together. Is it true?"

"Yeah," he said. "I'm going to play guitar. Bruce Patman will be on bass, and Scott Joslin on drums. Right now, we're working on 'Chocolate Kisses for My Baby.' "

"Wow," Brooke said less than enthusiastically, looking down at her feet. There were a few moments of uncomfortable silence.

"So," Colin said. "How's your article on Coco coming?"

"Uh, well, not so good. Actually I turned it over to Mandy Miller, because I didn't really have time for it," Brooke said. She could feel her cheeks turning red and she was glad that the bus drove up just then. *Was there any way to escape this?* she asked herself. Even the boy she liked talked constantly about her mother!

Bobby answered Brooke's knock on the door of the hotel suite. He was holding Sonya, and when Sonya saw Brooke, she giggled and held out her arms happily.

"Hi, Brooke," Bobby said. "You're just in time to give Sonya her afternoon snack."

Brooke settled her baby sister in her high chair and put some animal crackers on her tray while Bobby filled a bottle. "Where's Mom?" Brooke asked.

Bobby sighed. "Would you believe it? We

were having a wonderful, lazy morning, when Bernice called. Apparently Coco's new music video made such a splash that people are lined up begging for interviews." He grinned proudly. "Not only that, but she was asked to tape an unscheduled segment for the TV show *Star Talk* in Los Angeles. Isn't that great? With that kind of coverage, we can just watch her records climb the charts!"

Brooke frowned. "Mom's gone to L.A.? But we were all going to do something together this afternoon! When will she be back?"

Bobby looked uncomfortable. "That's what I'm trying to tell you, honey. She won't be back until—"

At that moment, the phone rang. Bobby answered it, then held out the phone to Brooke. "It's your mom," he said. "She wants to talk to you."

Brooke took the telephone. "I'm really sorry about tonight, Brooke," Mrs. Gray said. "I'm afraid I have to stay in the city. Bernice has scheduled another interview for—"

"But Mom," Brooke wailed, "Bobby *promised* that you'd be here!"

"I know, honey," Mrs. Gray said unhappily.

"But sometimes things don't work out the way we plan. Let's try again for tomorrow." Then she paused. "No, I'm sorry. I can't do it tomorrow, because Bernice has scheduled an interview in Santa Barbara. But I'll be in Sweet Valley on Thursday to sign autographs at Sweet Valley Disks. Maybe you could come to the hotel for dinner afterward."

"Thursday!" Brooke cried. "But that's two days away!"

"I'm sorry to disappoint you, sweetie," her mother said, "but it's the best I can do. How about it? Dinner on Thursday?"

"I guess," Brooke said glumly, and hung up.

Bobby gave Brooke a sympathetic look. "I know how you feel, Brooke, but your mother has feelings, too. I wish you would—"

"No, you *don't* know how I feel," Brooke interrupted him resentfully. There was a hard, painful lump in the middle of her stomach, and she slumped down on the sofa. "*Nobody* knows."

Bobby shook his head. "Hey, wait a sec," he said. "That's not true. If anybody knows what's going through your mind, it's me. *I* don't exist either, right?"

Brooke looked at him.

"And neither does Sonya," Bobby said, giving Sonya a little squeeze. "But we love her, and we're willing to put up with a lot to make sure that she gets what she deserves. She's worked very hard for this career and—"

Brooke stood up. "I don't care how hard she's worked," she said flatly. "She doesn't have to treat me this way. She's being completely unfair."

"I know you feel that way, honey," Bobby said, trying to console her. "All I'm saying is just hang in there a while longer—"

"If we hang in there, things are just going to get worse!" Brooke said. "Bernice wants Mom to be a big star, no matter how much it hurts *us*." She stormed to the door and yanked it open. "You may be willing to stand around and take it," she yelled, "but *I'm* not!" She slammed the door behind her as hard as she could.

"Is that this month's issue of *Smash*?" Ellen asked, sitting down next to Jessica on Wednesday morning before the bell rang for homeroom. "I hear they're running a story on Coco."

"Yeah," Jessica said, "but it's pretty disappointing." She laid the magazine on her desk for Ellen to look at. The headline on the article read,

"*Smash* Spills the Beans about Coco—the Fabulous French Treat!"

"It doesn't spill any beans," Jessica complained. "It doesn't say anything we didn't already know."

"Anyway, Coco's not French," Ellen protested, "she's American! Doesn't *Smash* know anything?"

"I wonder where she's from?" Jessica said. "I wonder if she has a boyfriend?"

Lila shrugged. "Maybe she's married," she said.

"Married?" Ellen scoffed. "Rock stars are never married."

Caroline Pearce leaned over from her seat across the aisle. "Didn't you hear the rumor about Coco and Johnny Buck?" she asked.

Jessica raised her eyebrows. "What?"

"I heard they're engaged," Caroline said importantly.

Brooke was walking past in the aisle and stopped. "Coco can't be engaged to Johnny Buck! She's already married. She—" She stopped suddenly.

"Sure, Brooke," Ellen said snidely. "Anyway, how would *you* know?"

Brooke flushed and looked down. Then she glared at Ellen and walked away.

Lila and Ellen looked at each other. "Uh-oh, it's the return of the old Brooke Dennis," Ellen whispered.

"Yeah," Lila said. "What's her problem? It's a good thing we never made her a Unicorn."

Sitting at her desk, Brooke longed to put her head down and sob. She shivered when she thought of how close she had come to telling her mother's secret. When she heard Caroline spreading that ridiculous rumor about Coco and Johnny Buck being engaged, the words had just popped out of her mouth. But when Ellen had taunted her so sarcastically, she had almost deliberately told the truth. She wanted to so badly! But if she had, her mother would be angry and hurt, and Bobby would be so disappointed in her. She didn't even want to think about what Bernice would do.

Trying not to ruin my mother's career is ruining my life, she thought miserably.

Six

◆

On Wednesday afternoon, Jessica was sitting in the kitchen finishing off a brownie and a glass of milk when a woman from OmniArtists called. "Hello, Jessica," she said. "I wanted to tell you that Coco will be in Sweet Valley tomorrow to sign autographs at Sweet Valley Disks. She would like you to be there as her special guest. Will you be able to come?"

"Of course I'll be there!" Jessica cried. "I wouldn't miss it for the world!" After she hung up, she called Lila, but Lila's phone was busy, so she called Mandy.

"That's great!" Mandy said, when she heard

the news. "All of the members of the fan club will want to come. We'll all wear our T-shirts."

"Good idea!" Jessica exclaimed. "We'll show Coco how much all the kids in Sweet Valley love her. In fact, we could give her the banner we made at Lila's house." She could just imagine the waves of applause that would fill the record shop when she presented the banner to Coco.

"All *right*!" Mandy agreed. "And Lila could bring her video camera and tape all of us with Coco."

"I'll call Lila right away," Jessica said.

"What was that all about?" Elizabeth asked as she walked into the kitchen with Amy.

"Guess what, you guys, Coco is coming to Sweet Valley tomorrow," Jessica said. "She's going to sign autographs at Sweet Valley Disks, and *I* get to be her special guest! The whole fan club's going," she added. "We're taking the banner we painted, and Lila's going to videotape the whole thing."

"Hey, that's terrific," Amy said. "Wow— Coco *herself*! I bet everybody will be there."

"It's kind of weird that Coco would hold an autograph party *here*," Elizabeth said thoughtfully.

"Sweet Valley isn't very big—wouldn't you think they'd hold it in L.A.?"

"Maybe it's because of the fan club," Jessica said. "After all, Coco Crazy *is* the first Coco fan club in this country!"

"Does Brooke know about this?" Amy asked. "This will be great for her *Sixers* article."

Elizabeth frowned. "It's really strange. Brooke turned over the article to Mandy. I don't know why. I tried to talk to her after math, but she didn't stop to talk after class. I looked for her at lunch but I couldn't find her."

"I saw her," Amy said. "She was sitting all by herself in the corner eating a sandwich, but when I went over to talk to her, she left. I kind of got the feeling she wanted to be alone."

"Well, if you ask me," Jessica said emphatically, "there's something wrong. She acted really weird in homeroom this morning."

"She's been acting weird all week," Amy added. "She didn't come to Lila's video party, either. I thought that was strange, because she likes Coco so much."

"Maybe it's got something to do with her mother," Elizabeth suggested. "Brooke told me that her mom and stepdad and little sister were moving back to California."

"But you'd think that would make her happy," Amy said.

"Sure, but maybe something has gone wrong. I'm going to call her later and ask her if she wants to come with us to Coco's autograph signing tomorrow. Maybe that will cheer her up."

The news about Coco's appearance at Sweet Valley Disks spread like wildfire around school on Thursday morning. Everybody was planning to go—everybody but Elizabeth and Brooke.

"I can't believe you're not going to Coco's autograph signing," Amy complained at lunch.

Elizabeth sighed. "Me, either. But I promised Mr. Bowman I'd stay after school and finish the layout of the next issue of *The Sixers*."

"And Brooke's not coming either?" Amy asked.

Elizabeth shook her head. "She said she couldn't make it."

Amy frowned. "Did she say why?"

"No," Elizabeth said. "She didn't want to talk about it. She walked away before we were finished talking."

It was nearly four-thirty when Elizabeth left

school that afternoon and walked to Brooke's house. There were actually two reasons Elizabeth hadn't gone to the autograph signing. The first was *The Sixers*, but the second was that she wanted to go over and talk to Brooke. She hadn't been able to talk to her at school and she was really beginning to worry about her friend. Mr. Dennis answered her knock at the door. "Hello, Elizabeth," he said. "Brooke is up in her room. She's going to have dinner with her mother, but you have plenty of time for a visit."

The door to Brooke's room was partly open, and Elizabeth tapped on it. "It's Elizabeth," she called. She lightly pushed the door open and stepped in. "Your dad said you—"

"Elizabeth!" Brooke exclaimed, jumping up from her bed. "I didn't expect—I didn't expect company."

"Are you OK?" Elizabeth asked gently. "I've had the feeling all week that something's been bothering you."

Brooke hunched her shoulders. "Nothing's wrong," she mumbled. "I'm fine."

Elizabeth frowned. She looked up and noticed Coco's poster on the wall above Brooke's bed. She looked quickly from Brooke's face to Coco's. No wonder Jessica thought that Coco looked familiar. "You know what, Brooke," she said. "I just realized that you look a lot like Coco."

Brooke sat down on the bed with her head hanging. "If . . . if I tell you something," she said brokenly, "will you promise not to tell anyone? Not my father, not Jessica, not anybody."

Elizabeth hesitated. "I promise," she said.

"You probably won't believe this, but I swear it's true. The thing is . . . I mean, Coco is—" Brooke stopped and swallowed hard. "You see, Elizabeth, Coco is my mom."

"Your mom?" she asked numbly.

"I know it sounds weird," Brooke said, "but it's true."

"Nobody knows this? Not even your dad?"

Brooke shook her head. "I'm not supposed to tell him—not yet, at least." She gestured toward the poster. "If I keep my door shut he almost never comes in my room."

"But why do you have to keep it a secret?" Elizabeth asked.

"Mom's agent—this woman named Bernice— thinks that Coco's career as a rock star would be ruined if people found out that she has a family. As far as the world is concerned, Bobby and

Sonya and I don't exist." Her brown eyes filled with tears. "It's *awful*, Elizabeth!"

Elizabeth sat down beside Brooke on the bed. "Oh, Brooke," she said sympathetically. "It sounds terrible. It probably doesn't help that everybody at school talks about Coco all the time."

Brooke nodded, wiping her eyes. "It's almost impossible not to give everything away." Brooke sighed. "But that's not even the worst thing, Elizabeth. The worst is that my mom puts her work ahead of everything—including *me*. Every time I plan to see her she has another interview. Right now, when we could be together, she's at Sweet Valley Disks signing autographs."

"Why didn't you go?"

"Would you like to watch everybody rave about your mother and have to pretend you don't know her?"

"I guess not," Elizabeth admitted. "But you're having dinner with her tonight, aren't you? That's what your dad said."

"Yeah, sure," Brooke said. "Big deal. I get to go to the Sweet Valley Plaza and order room service, because my mom's agent is scared that somebody might recognize her if we went out together."

Elizabeth wasn't sure what to say. Brooke's mother had given her a very difficult task—to pretend that she wasn't Coco's daughter while all Brooke's friends were going Coco crazy.

"What an incredible afternoon!" Lila said to Jessica.

"It's unbelievable, isn't it?" Jessica said happily, looking around at the noisy crowd of kids at Sweet Valley Disks.

The autograph-signing party was even better than Jessica had imagined. She had worn her T-shirt, jeans, red cowboy boots, and fringed jacket, and as president of Coco Crazy, she had stood right beside Coco all afternoon. Coco was completely cool, laughing and joking and writing something personal with every autograph. She'd made an enormous hit with the kids. And the fan club had sold three dozen T-shirts!

Jessica sighed. There was only one thing about the afternoon that had been less than perfect. She had really been hoping to find out a little about Coco's life. As she stood beside her, Jessica tried to ask her questions, but Coco gave a few very vague answers, and Jessica felt like she didn't know anything more than she had before. *Is she hiding something?* Jessica asked herself. As she stood there trying to think of a way to find out more about her idol, she felt someone tap on her shoulder. She turned around to see Colin.

"Jessica," he said, "have you seen Brooke?"

Jessica shook her head. "Elizabeth told me she wasn't coming this afternoon."

"I wonder why. I know she's a big fan of Coco's."

Lila tossed her brown hair and laughed. "Brooke Dennis?" she interrupted. "She's not a fan of anybody but herself."

At that moment Coco walked over. "Do you mind if I talk to Jessica for a minute?" she asked.

Jessica noticed Lila eyeing her enviously.

"Jessica," Coco said when they were alone, "I want to thank you for being such a wonderful fan. This has been a terrific afternoon." She glanced up at the big WE LOVE COCO banner that hung on the wall. "You and your friends went to a lot of work to get all the members of the fan club here, and I appreciate it."

"It was nothing," Jessica said modestly. "We'd do it again in a second."

Coco smiled. "You've done so much for me

that I'd like to do something in return." She handed Jessica an envelope. "Here are two tickets for front-row seats to my concert next Saturday night."

"Your concert?" Jessica gasped.

"It was just arranged this morning," Coco said with a look of excitement on her face. "The Boys Next Door were scheduled to play in the arena, but they had to cancel and my agent arranged for me to fill in. I hope that you and the rest of the fan club will be there."

"That's awesome!" Jessica exclaimed. "I can't wait! Of course we'll be there!"

A tall thin woman walked over to them. "There you are," she said impatiently to Coco. "There's a car waiting outside to take us back to the Sweet Valley Plaza."

Coco looked back at Jessica and smiled. "Good-bye, Jessica," she said. "I'll see you next Saturday. Don't forget."

"Oh, I won't forget," Jessica said as she watched Coco and the woman walk out of the store. Jessica stood there for a few moments deep in thought. She looked quickly around the store and hurried out the door.

* * *

At the Sweet Valley Plaza, Jessica paused at the registration desk and stepped forward. "I'd like Coco's room number, please," she said.

"Coco who?" the young woman behind the desk asked.

Jessica hesitated. "Uh . . . just Coco," she said.

The woman frowned. "I don't think we have a guest by that name," she said, "but hold on a moment and I'll check." A minute later she turned back to the counter. "I'm sorry," she said. "No one is registered under that name. Perhaps you have the wrong hotel."

Jessica thanked the woman and walked away. She knew she had the right hotel. Coco must be traveling under a different name, she decided. Or maybe she was using her *real* name! Wouldn't it be amazing if she could find out what it was?

Just then, out of the corner of her eye, Jessica caught a glimpse of Coco and the tall woman she had been with at the record store walking across the hotel lobby. Jessica leapt behind a pillar and watched as the two women went into an elevator. The floor indicator above the elevator began to light up—one, two, three, four, five. The elevator stopped on the fifth floor. Jessica dashed for the stairs.

As she ran up one flight of stairs after another, Jessica kept telling herself that she shouldn't be doing this—she shouldn't be sneaking around and spying on people. Besides, she told herself, speedily rounding the fourth floor landing, there was no way she could catch them anyway. But when she got to the fifth floor, panting and out of breath, she was delighted to find that Coco and the woman were still standing in the hallway, in front of a door marked 505. Jessica hid around the corner and listened.

"I don't think we're doing the right thing, Bernice," Coco was saying intently. "This secrecy—it's too hard on everybody."

Secrecy? Jessica thought, her ears perking up.

"I know it's hard," she heard the other woman say. "But if you'll just be patient a little longer—"

"But when will it end?" Coco asked in a voice that sounded sad to Jessica. "Look, I know we can't settle this tonight, and I'm tired. But we *have* to resolve this, and the sooner the better." She paused for a moment. "I'll see you for dinner in an hour—OK?"

"OK," the other woman said. Jessica peeked around the corner and watched her walk toward the elevator. Coco knocked on the door of Suite 505. "Bobby," she called softly. "It's Constance."

Jessica sucked in her breath. *Constance.* That was Coco's real name! Constance what? And who was Bobby?

A man—Bobby, she guessed—opened the door, holding a little girl in his arms. "Hi," he said with a grin. "Sonya and I have been wondering what was keeping you."

Coco held out her arms with a smile. "Come to Mommy, Sonya," she said, and took the little girl.

Jessica leaned against the wall. Coco—the rock star, her idol—must be married to Bobby, she realized, and Sonya must be their daughter.

Coco was a *mother*!

Seven

◆

When Brooke arrived at the Sweet Valley Plaza that evening for dinner she ran into Jessica Wakefield coming out of the elevator.

Brooke stood there startled. "H—Hi, Jessica."

"Uh . . . Hi, Brooke," Jessica said. She looked just as uncomfortable as Brooke felt. After an awkward moment, Brooke just waved and hurried into the elevator.

That was strange, she said to herself as she walked down the hall and knocked at the door of Suite 505.

Her mom greeted her at the door with a big hug. Brooke noticed she was still in her Coco costume from the autograph signing. "So how did it go this afternoon?" Brooke asked as her mom led her into the living room.

"It was terrific," Mrs. Gray said enthusiastically. "The entire fan club was there, and they brought a banner that said—"

"Not the *entire* fan club," Brooke pointed out. "*I* wasn't there."

"I know you weren't, honey," her mother said gently. "I wish you could have come, but Bernice thought it would be too awkward for you. I think she was right, don't you?"

"I guess," Brooke said.

"So the kids made a banner, huh?" Bobby asked. "That was nice. What did it say?"

Mrs. Gray smiled "It said 'We Love Coco' in big red letters, and it was signed by all the members of the fan club." She looked at Brooke. "Almost all," she corrected herself with a little smile.

Brooke sighed. The whole thing was too depressing to think about. "Let's change the subject," she suggested, trying to sound cheerful. "I had a great idea I wanted us to talk about."

Bobby looked up from the room service menu he was studying. "Oh, yeah?" he said. "I'm all for great ideas. Let's hear it."

Brooke leaned forward. "I was thinking that maybe we could all go away someplace where nobody knows Coco and do some *real* things for a change, like go roller-skating and swim in the ocean." She made a face. "It's getting pretty boring, just hanging around the hotel room."

"I'm with you, Brooke," Bobby said. "That sounds like a wonderful idea." He grinned at Mrs. Gray. "How about it, Constance? Maybe we could drive up to Big Sur. I know this great bed-and-breakfast right on the beach. We could ride horses and play in the tide pools and—"

Mrs. Gray shook her head regretfully. "I hate to tell you two this, but I'm not free this weekend."

"Hey!" Bobby said, frowning. "What happened to the weekend of rest and relaxation we had talked about? You've been working nonstop. This is supposed to be a *vacation*, remember?"

"I know that's what we planned," Mrs. Gray said ruefully, "but something has come up."

"I'll bet it has," Brooke said under her breath, but loud enough for everyone to hear.

Mrs. Gray pretended that she hadn't heard. "Bernice has scheduled a concert here in Sweet Valley for next Saturday, and—"

"Here?" Brooke exclaimed, dismayed. If her mom was giving a concert here, everybody at school would be obsessed with it. It would be even more impossible than it was before to get through school without giving away her secret.

"But I thought you weren't going to do any concerts for another few months," Bobby said. "I thought you were going to take some time to choose your backup, put an act together—"

"That's what I thought, too," Mrs. Gray said. Then she smiled. "But Bernice found out today that the Boys Next Door had to cancel their concert next Saturday. The promoter asked her if I was available and—" She lifted her arms in a triumphant gesture. "Voilà! Our first concert!"

"Yippee," Brooke said grimly.

"Hey, come on," Mrs. Gray protested. "This concert is a big deal, you guys! It's an incredible break for me. We're supposed to be *happy* about it."

Bobby got up and gave her a hug. "It's terrific, Constance," he said warmly. "We're just a little surprised, that's all. I thought we were going to have some time to ourselves for a change. But I'm really happy for you." He turned to Brooke.

"Hey, Brooke, isn't it terrific? Just think—your mother's giving her first U.S. concert right here in Sweet Valley!"

Brooke folded her arms. "Yeah, sure," she said sarcastically. "It's great. And what am I supposed to do? Hang out in my bedroom that night? Or go to the concert with a bag over my head and a big sign that says 'I don't exist'?"

Mrs. Gray sat down on the sofa. "Brooke," she said tenderly. "I wish you wouldn't—"

"Wouldn't what, Mom?" Brooke said angrily. She jumped up from the sofa. "Wouldn't hang around and embarrass you by wanting people to know that you're my mom? Do you want me just to disappear? Am I supposed to hide from my friends forever, so I don't accidentally give away the terrible secret that you're my mother?"

Bobby frowned. "Brooke," he said sternly, "you know your mom doesn't want anything like that. She wants you to be happy."

"Bobby's right, honey," Mrs. Gray said. She held out her hand to Brooke. "More than anything I want you to be happy."

"Then let's go away for the weekend, Mom," Brooke pleaded desperately. She sat down on the sofa again. "Big Sur is so pretty this time of year. We could play in the sand and swim and eat great food and—"

"It sounds wonderful, Brooke, but I'm afraid it's out of the question," Mrs. Gray said softly. "I just can't pass up this opportunity. The concert is only a week away, and there's an incredible amount of work to do. We have to get the band together, get costumes, rehearse—" She shook her head. "Starting Monday we'll probably be rehearsing constantly."

Brooke looked at her mother. "I guess this means that I can forget about going away together, and I can forget about seeing you at all."

Mrs. Gray sighed. "I'd hoped we'd be able to be together every day, sweetheart. That's why Bobby and I came to Sweet Valley. Unfortunately, with the concert, it looks like there won't be much private time for a little while." She managed a smile. "But it will all be worth it in the end, believe me. When all this is over, you'll be glad that you put up with the inconvenience."

"Mom—" Brooke began, but she was interrupted by Bernice, who had come into the room without knocking.

"You should listen to your mother, Brooke,"

Bernice said firmly. "She's telling you the truth. If this concert goes well, Coco's career could skyrocket. Things could *really* begin to get exciting!"

Brooke glanced at Bernice. "What do you mean by really exciting?" she asked.

"A big concert tour. *Nothing* is more exciting than a star's first major tour."

"A tour?" Brooke asked. "You mean she'd be traveling around the United States?"

"Of course Coco will have an American tour," Bernice answered. "But I'm thinking of a *world* tour. If Coco's as big a success as I think she'll be, she'll soon be singing in all the important cities of the world! London, Paris, Tokyo, Hong Kong—you name it!"

Brooke swung around to face her mother. "And what does that mean for me? Does that mean I get to see you for a few hours between world tours, when you happen to stop in Sweet Valley to sign a few more autographs?"

"I know you're upset, Brooke, and I understand why. All I'm asking for is a little patience," her mother pleaded. She held out her hand. "After next weekend, things will get better, I promise."

"It's easy to make promises," Brooke said,

ignoring her mother's hand. "It's a lot harder to keep them." She marched out of the hotel room and shut the door behind her.

"Where have you been, Jessica?" Mrs. Wakefield asked, as Jessica came into the kitchen. "It's late."

"I'm sorry, Mom," Jessica said, looking down. "I . . . I had to pick up something from Lila's after Coco's autograph party."

"Well, if it isn't our own little Coco," Steven said, walking into the kitchen. "Hey," he teased, "how did it feel, rubbing elbows with a star?"

"It felt pretty good," Jessica replied distractedly. She was thinking about the scene she had just witnessed at the hotel.

"Just pretty good?" Steven asked.

Jessica looked up. "Actually, it felt great. Especially when she gave me two front-row tickets to her concert next Saturday night."

Steven looked impressed. "Way to go, shrimp," he said. "Two, huh? One for you and one for me?"

Jessica laughed. "Don't count on it."

She grabbed an apple and headed for her room. Normally when she had a piece of big news like this, she headed immediately for the phone to call Lila or Ellen or one of the other Unicorns.

But Jessica didn't feel comfortable running to the phone with this news. *For one thing, I was snooping when I found it out.* She told herself as she took off her fringed jacket and flopped down on her bed. *For another thing it's obvious that Coco has gone to a lot of trouble to keep anyone from finding out about her family*, she thought. *But why is she hiding it?* she asked herself. Somehow she didn't feel right telling her friends what she'd discovered until she knew the answer to that question. Of course, there was one person she felt safe telling.

"Hi, Lizzie," Jessica said, walking through the bathroom to her twin's room and sitting down on her bed.

"Hi, Jess, what's up?" Elizabeth asked.

Jessica hesitated for a few moments. "Elizabeth, what would you do if somebody famous had a secret they were trying to keep from the whole world, and you discovered it?"

Elizabeth turned around and stared at her for a moment. "So you found out about Coco?"

Jessica stared back in puzzlement. "How did you know?"

"How did *you* know?" Elizabeth asked.

Jessica blushed and didn't say anything.

"Listen, Jess," Elizabeth said urgently. "You can't tell anyone about this. If anyone finds out Brooke is Coco's daughter, she could get in a lot of trouble."

"What?" Jessica shouted. "Brooke Dennis is Coco's daughter?" She thought back to the awkward moment when she ran into Brooke at the Sweet Valley Plaza.

Elizabeth groaned. "I have a feeling I just gave away a very big secret. If you didn't know that, then what were you trying to tell me?"

Suddenly Jessica felt very silly. "Elizabeth, this was really horrible of me, but I followed Coco to her hotel after the autograph party. I found out that she has a husband named Bobby and a little girl named Sonya. But I didn't know anything about Brooke!"

"Nobody is supposed to know," Elizabeth said.

"Why not?" Jessica asked. "If my mom were a rock star, I'd want everyone to know."

"It's not that Brooke doesn't want to tell," Elizabeth explained, "she isn't allowed to tell. Coco's agent thinks it would hurt her career if people found out that Coco's married and has two children."

Jessica frowned. "I guess I can't think of any really big stars who have kids," she said slowly. "But how awful for Brooke! It doesn't seem fair somehow. No wonder Brooke has seemed so miserable lately!"

Elizabeth nodded. "Promise me you won't tell anyone about this, Jessica. The truth would be all over Sweet Valley in a few hours, and the newspapers and television would pick it up right away. Brooke has done everything she can to keep this a secret. It would be terrible if she got blamed for the whole world finding out."

"You look as if you're worried about something, honey," Brooke's father said to her at breakfast the next morning. He frowned a little. "Does it have something to do with your mom? You haven't been spending as much time with her as I had expected."

Brooke bit her lip. She wanted more than anything to tell him the truth. But she'd promised she wouldn't. "It's nothing, Dad. I'm a little down, that's all. Don't worry."

Mr. Dennis leaned over and put his hand on Brooke's arm. "You know that you can talk to me if you want, don't you, sweetheart? If you're having problems in school or with your mother—anything. I'd like to help."

"Thanks, Dad," Brooke said, avoiding his eyes. She pushed her chair back and stood up. "I've got to hurry or I'll be late for school."

Mr. Dennis got up, too. "How about a ride to school this morning?"

Brooke shook her head. "No, thanks. I'd rather walk."

The truth was that she wanted to be alone to think. She had said so many things last night and felt so awful. When she'd gotten home from the hotel she'd gone straight to her room and cried. When her father knocked on her door later to tell her her mother was on the phone, she had pretended to be asleep.

Things were getting worse and worse. Her mother's career was going to take off like a skyrocket if Bernice got her way, and Brooke wasn't sure she could handle it. More than anything, Brooke just wanted her mom back.

Brooke thought desperately about what to do

all the way to school and throughout her morning classes. At the beginning of lunch period she was walking past the telephone outside the principal's office, when she stopped. Without allowing herself to think for a moment longer, she took a deep breath and dialed information.

"The number for the *Sweet Valley Tribune*, please," she said.

A few seconds later her hand trembled as she dialed the number.

"I'd like to speak to the entertainment editor," she said.

A moment later a man came on the line. "Tom Reynolds," he said.

"My name is Brooke Dennis," Brooke said, and spelled it for him. "I, uh, I called because I have a story for you. Uh . . . you see . . . I'm Coco's daughter."

There was a moment of silence. "*Whose* daughter?" Mr. Reynolds asked.

"The rock star, Coco. She's my mother," Brooke said patiently. "She's married and has another daughter named Sonya who's a year old. Her real name is Constance Gray."

Mr. Reynolds cleared his throat. "You'll excuse

me if I'm a little surprised," he said. "It isn't every day that we get a story like this over the phone. Do you mind if I ask a few questions?"

It took five minutes to answer Mr. Reynolds's questions and convince him she knew what she was talking about. "Uh, when do you think you'll print this information?" Brooke asked.

"I can't say for sure," Mr. Reynolds replied. "I have to check it out, of course. It sounds like you're telling the truth, but for all I know, it might be a hoax. If the facts check out, you can expect to read your story next week sometime. Stay tuned."

"Believe me, I will," Brooke said, and hung up the phone.

Eight

◇

"Jessica," Mrs. Wakefield said, coming into the kitchen on Friday afternoon. "Mrs. Pearce mentioned something to me today that I need to ask you about."

Jessica snapped her head up. *This is it*, she thought.

Just then the phone rang and her mother picked it up. "Nancy, hi!" Mrs. Wakefield said. "What a nice surprise."

Jessica breathed a sigh of relief. *Saved by the bell*, she thought. It was her mother's sister, Nancy. She knew they'd talk for hours. She took the opportunity to run out of the kitchen and up the stairs.

She went first to Steven's room. "Steven," she hissed. "Emergency meeting in my room." Then she yanked Elizabeth into her room. When all three were gathered she shut the door.

"Listen," she said, "I'm pretty sure Mom has figured out about the party. Or at least she's about to. She just said that she wants to talk to me about something Mrs. Pearce told her. Luckily the phone rang and I escaped."

Steven groaned. "We're goners."

"I knew this was going to happen!" Elizabeth said.

"What should we do?" Jessica asked.

"Maybe we should just confess and get it over with," Elizabeth suggested.

"What do you think they'll do to us if we confess?" Jessica asked fearfully.

"What do you think they'll do if we don't?" Steven said.

After a long pause, Steven spoke again. "I vote we tell," he said.

"Right now?" Jessica asked.

"Right now," Elizabeth said. "Before we lose our nerve."

"Jessica!" she heard her mom yell from downstairs.

Great, Jessica thought. "Here we go," she muttered.

The three of them trooped downstairs and found their mother drinking a cup of tea in the kitchen. She raised her eyebrows when she saw the three of them together.

"Mom," Steven said, "we have something to tell you. We, uh . . . we . . ." He examined his shoes for a while and then looked over at Elizabeth. "Elizabeth will explain."

Elizabeth rolled her eyes. "Mom, while you and Dad were in Mexico we . . . well we—"

"—had a few friends over," Jessica broke in hurriedly. "Not a lot—well, not a *whole* lot."

"The thing is, we didn't ask permission, so it's kind of been on our minds, you know?" Steven said.

"Hmmmm," Mrs. Wakefield said. "Some friends over, huh? That wouldn't happen to explain where the pickles went, would it?"

Elizabeth nodded. "The mayonnaise, too."

"And that's where the extra trash came from," Steven explained. "We cleaned everything up, though."

"Except the bologna in my shoe," Mrs. Wakefield said.

"We did miss a few things," Jessica said, biting her lip.

Mrs. Wakefield frowned. "What about May? Did she agree to your having this—these friends over?"

Elizabeth blushed. "Not exactly," she said. "She . . . uh, she—"

"—had errands to do on Saturday," Jessica finished. "She had a lot of errands. By the time she got back, almost everybody was gone."

"We did all the cleaning up ourselves," Steven added.

"I see," Mrs. Wakefield said. She was silent for a moment, looking first at Steven, then at Elizabeth, and finally at Jessica. "I'm surprised at you three," she said. "You should have known better than to have friends over without parental supervision, especially when your father and I trusted you to act responsibly while we were gone. Something terrible could have happened."

"What are you going to . . . do?" Jessica asked.

Mrs. Wakefield shook her head. "I don't know yet. I need to talk to your father about it. He and I will discuss it and decide what should be done."

Steven, Elizabeth, and Jessica all nodded their heads solemnly and turned to leave the room.

"Oh, by the way, Jessica," Mrs. Wakefield said. "Mrs. Pearce wanted me to talk to you about making signs for the neighborhood garage sale. She said you did a wonderful job on ours."

On Monday morning Brooke got up early, ran downstairs, and grabbed the *Sweet Valley Tribune* off the front steps. Holding her breath, she scanned the front page for the story about Coco. She sighed with relief when she realized it wasn't there. She quickly turned to the Arts and Entertainment section and riffled through the pages. Still nothing. They hadn't printed the story yet, and she was spared until tomorrow. She brought the newspaper to the kitchen table and went upstairs to get dressed.

She dreaded to think what would happen when the story came out. She had spent the weekend by herself feeling ashamed of what she'd done. Elizabeth and Jessica had invited her to the movies on Saturday, but she had pretended to be busy. Brooke couldn't bear to talk about what she'd done, and she couldn't think about anything else.

She knew that Bernice would be furious, but that wasn't what mattered. Bobby would be disappointed in her, and her mother—what would her mother think?

When Brooke arrived at school, she was surprised to see Colin Harmon waiting for her at her locker. "Hi, Brooke," he said. Colin seemed very nervous.

"Hi," she said.

"Uh, Brooke . . . I was wondering if—" he paused and looked down. "I was wondering—well, I got two tickets to Coco's concert on Saturday night. I was wondering if maybe . . . uh, you wanted to go with me?" He looked up at her.

Brooke couldn't meet his eyes. It was all too awful. She had just been asked on the first date of her whole life by a boy she really liked—and it was to her mother's concert.

Colin was going to find out the truth about Coco soon enough, just like everybody else, Brooke reasoned. What would he think of her when he found out what she had just done to her mother's career? He would probably think she was awful, just like everybody else.

"Brooke?" Colin said, interrupting her thoughts.

"Thank you for asking me, Colin," Brooke said. "But I can't go. I don't think my mom would let me."

"Have you heard?" Caroline Pearce shrieked, running up to Elizabeth as soon as she arrived at school on Friday morning. "Ellen Riteman said that she heard that Aaron Dallas said that he saw an article in the newspaper this morning that said that Coco is *Brooke Dennis's mother*! Can you believe that?"

"I'd like to see a copy of the newspaper," Elizabeth said evenly. Caroline went racing off to tell somebody else the news. *What is going on?* Elizabeth wondered.

Amy came up to Elizabeth at her locker. "Elizabeth!" she exclaimed. "Did you hear about Brooke?"

"Caroline just told me," Elizabeth said. "Did you see the paper?"

"Aaron Dallas brought a copy to school. Pretty amazing, huh?"

Elizabeth nodded. "Have you seen Brooke?"

"No," Amy said.

"I'm going to try to find her before homeroom," Elizabeth said.

When Elizabeth finally found Brooke near the water fountain, she was so mobbed by Unicorns and other admirers that Elizabeth couldn't even get near her. And Brooke didn't look very happy about all the attention. *Poor Brooke*, Elizabeth thought.

At lunch that day the entire cafeteria was buzzing with the news.

"Can you *believe* it?" Ellen gushed. "Coco is Brooke's mom. It's just too amazing."

"I can't believe Brooke kept it a secret," Lila said incredulously.

"Brooke is *sooo* lucky," Janet Howell said.

Jessica glanced down at the newspaper lying in the middle of the lunch table. *How well do you know your favorite star?* the front-page headline of the Arts section demanded. The story took up two columns and included three pictures: one of Sonya and Bobby snapped at the hotel swimming pool, one of Coco, and one of Brooke.

"I think I'll throw a big party to celebrate Coco's concert," Lila said importantly, "and Brooke will be the guest of honor. Maybe she could get Coco to come!"

"I'm surprised we didn't guess about Brooke

and Coco," Ellen said thoughtfully. "I mean they look so much alike, and Brooke has been acting so weird lately."

"And we all knew Brooke's mom lived in Paris and was in Sweet Valley for a visit," Janet said.

"Yeah," Lila said. "We definitely should have figured it out. Boy, Jessica, I bet you feel pretty dumb. You're the president of Coco Crazy, and even *you* didn't know!"

Brooke had lived through some pretty miserable days in the past few weeks, but this one was the very worst. People had crowded around her all day long, asking stupid questions about her mother, demanding autographed pictures, tickets to the concert, and backstage passes. Suddenly the Unicorns were her best friends. Lila even wanted to throw a party for her! Everybody seemed to want something. And everybody seemed to think that having a rock star for a mother was the most wonderful thing in the world. *If only they knew*, she thought.

By the time the last bell rang she was snapping at everybody and had told at least a few to get lost. All she wanted to do was get away from school as quickly as possible. *I'm not sure I can handle this,* she thought miserably.

She was surprised at how glad she felt to see Elizabeth waiting for her at her locker. She needed to talk to somebody, and she knew that if anyone would understand it was Elizabeth.

"Do you want to walk home together?" Elizabeth asked.

"More than anything," Brooke said gratefully.

Nine

◇

As Brooke and Elizabeth walked home, Brooke explained to Elizabeth why she had leaked the story to the newspaper, and how afraid she was of what her mother would do when she found out.

"It's not that I don't want my mom's career to be a success. I do," Brooke explained. "It's just that all the lying is too hard. And I'm afraid if Bernice gets her way I'll lose my mom forever. I felt like if I didn't do something my whole life would be ruined."

Elizabeth nodded sympathetically.

"But now that I gave the newspaper the story I feel terrible," Brooke said. "I thought nothing could be more awful than having to keep my mom's identity a secret, but I realized today that having everyone know is even worse."

They had almost reached Brooke's house when a shiny black car pulled up beside them. The window whirred open, and Brooke saw that it was Bernice. She felt her stomach pull into a painful knot. "Uh-oh," Brooke said softly.

"It's my mother's agent," Brooke whispered to Elizabeth.

"Brooke, I need to speak with you. Get in the car," Bernice commanded brusquely.

"You don't have to go with her if you don't want to," Elizabeth whispered back.

Brooke sighed. The last thing in the world she wanted to do was get in that car. But she turned to Elizabeth and tried to muster a brave face. "I knew something like this was going to happen. I might as well get it over with." Brooke whispered as she opened the passenger door.

Elizabeth watched her worriedly. "Brooke, call me as soon as you get home," she said.

"OK," Brooke said, and got in the car. She saw Elizabeth watching them with concern as they pulled away from the curb.

Bernice drove the few blocks to Brooke's

house, stopped the car across the street, and switched off the engine.

She turned to Brooke and gave her a long look. "I suppose you're the one who's responsible for the story in the paper this morning."

"Yes," Brooke said quietly.

"I don't understand you! You're not even trying to deny what you've done?"

"No," Brooke said, quieter still.

"Don't you see what you've done to your mother?" Bernice demanded angrily. "Don't you know how important her career is to her?"

"My mother's important to *me*, too," Brooke burst out. "If she becomes a big star, the way you want, I'll never get to be with her! She'll be in foreign cities on tour, or giving interviews, or signing autographs."

"I can't believe how selfish you're being," Bernice said between clenched teeth. "All you're thinking about is yourself."

"That's not true," Brooke cried. "I'm thinking about my mom! We've had to be apart ever since you told her she should move to France. She moved back to California so we could all be together. If her career takes off, we'll be apart forever."

Bernice gave a short laugh. "And that's not being selfish? You're acting like you're the only important thing in your mother's life."

Brooke could feel the tears stinging her eyes. "But I'm her daughter," she whispered.

"Think of it this way, Brooke," Bernice said. "Your mom is important to you. But you've also got your dad, your school, your friends—all of them are important, too. If your mom asked you to give them up, you'd be miserable. Isn't that so?"

Brooke nodded numbly.

"Well, it's the same for your mother," Bernice said. "She could never be happy if she had to give up singing or Bobby or Sonya—just to be with you. Do you understand?"

Brooke nodded again, blinking back the tears.

Bernice reached over and opened the door. "I want you to go home and think about the damage you've done. I haven't spoken to your mother yet, but I'm *sure* she's going to be furious." She paused. "I think it would be better if you didn't tell her about our little conversation," she said. "She has a lot on her mind right now, and she doesn't need to worry about you."

Brooke nodded and climbed out of the car.

As she stood on the curb watching Bernice drive away, Brooke was blinded by tears. *Bernice is right,* she thought miserably. *I wasn't thinking of my mother and what would make her happy. Now she'll be miserable, and it's all my fault!*

Brooke walked into the house. She couldn't undo what she had done. But there was one thing she could do to make sure she never hurt her mother again.

She could disappear.

"Elizabeth," Mrs. Wakefield said, poking her head into Elizabeth's room that evening. "Mr. Dennis is downstairs. He wants to talk to you."

"Mr. Dennis?" Elizabeth asked in surprise. She rushed down the stairs.

Mr. Dennis was waiting in the living room looking very agitated. "Hi, Elizabeth," he said. "I came to ask you if you had seen Brooke this afternoon. She hasn't come home yet, and I'm starting to get a little nervous."

"Brooke and I walked home together from school this afternoon," Elizabeth told him. "But just before we got to your house, her mother's agent, Bernice, drove up and wanted to talk with Brooke. Bernice seemed pretty mad," Elizabeth continued. "I was worried, so I told Brooke to call me when she got home, but she still hasn't called."

Mr. Dennis was shaking his head. "Well, neither Bernice nor Constance know where she is now. I just spoke to them." He stood up and began to pace across the living room. "I didn't know what was going on with Brooke's mother until today. I can't believe Constance would put such a burden on Brooke. Trying to keep all those secrets has been terrible for her. I really wish I had known."

Elizabeth nodded.

"I could tell Brooke has been unhappy lately, but I couldn't figure out why," Mr. Dennis continued. "I asked her to talk to me, but she wouldn't. Now I realize it was because she couldn't." Mr. Dennis stopped pacing and sat down again.

"My suspicion is that Bernice got very angry at Brooke for the story in the newspaper," he said. "From the look of her room, I'm afraid Brooke has run away."

Elizabeth nodded. "I know she was feeling terrible even before she talked to Bernice."

"I think I had better call the police," Mr. Dennis said grimly. "I don't know what else to do.

I've already called Amy Sutton, Julie Porter, and Mandy Miller, and nobody has seen her. Elizabeth, exactly what time did Brooke get in the car with Bernice?"

"About three-fifteen," Elizabeth replied.

"Can you suggest anyone else I could call?"

Elizabeth thought for a moment and shook her head.

"Thank you for your help, Elizabeth," Mr. Dennis said, heading for the door.

An hour later, Steven came to find Elizabeth to tell her that Constance Gray was on the phone for her.

Coco! Elizabeth thought, and ran to the hall phone.

"Elizabeth, I just spoke to Brooke's father, and he said you were the last to see Brooke," Mrs. Gray said urgently.

"Actually your agent, Bernice, was the last to see her," Elizabeth explained.

"And what exactly happened with Bernice?" Mrs. Gray asked. Elizabeth detected a lot of anger in her voice.

"She pulled up in a car and told Brooke to get in. She said she needed to speak with her.

She looked really mad, and I could tell Brooke was nervous," Elizabeth said.

"It makes me *furious* that Bernice yelled at my daughter!" Mrs. Gray said, suddenly unable to contain her anger. There were a few moments of silence. "I hope you'll excuse me, Elizabeth," Mrs. Gray said. "I'm very upset. I realize how difficult all this has been on Brooke, and I feel terrible. I don't know what I'll do if anything happens to her. If you hear anything from her, you'll let me or her father know, won't you?"

"I will," Elizabeth promised.

"In the meantime I've cancelled my concert tomorrow night. I can't possibly concentrate on anything but finding Brooke right now," Mrs. Gray said. "I hope she comes home."

"Me, too," Elizabeth said.

Elizabeth ran to Jessica as soon as she got home from the movies that evening. "Jessica," she said urgently. "Brooke has disappeared. I think she's run away."

Jessica's eyes widened. "Run away?"

"Her father came here to ask if I'd seen her, and then her mom called after that. They're both frantic."

"*Coco* called?" Jessica asked.

"Yeah," Elizabeth said. "You haven't heard anything from Brooke, have you?"

Jessica shook her head.

"Poor Brooke!" Elizabeth exclaimed. "It's been hours and hours since anybody saw her. Where *is* she?"

"I'm sure she's all right," Jessica said comfortingly. "Maybe she went to stay with a friend."

"Without telling anyone?" Elizabeth said. "Anyway, her dad called all her friends, and nobody knows where she is."

"She'll turn up," Jessica said as she headed into the kitchen.

Why is Jessica being so calm about this? Elizabeth couldn't help wondering.

The next morning when Elizabeth came downstairs there was a note from her parents on the kitchen table saying they had gone to play tennis. Steven had stayed overnight at Joe Howell's house, so she and Jessica were alone for breakfast.

She also noticed that one of her parents had cut out an article from the paper and left it on the table. "Star's daughter disappears," the headline proclaimed. Under that was a smaller headline: "Distraught Coco says no concert unless daughter is found." There was a picture of Brooke. Elizabeth guessed Brooke's parents gave the story to the *Tribune* in the hope that somebody would see Brooke and give them some information.

After Elizabeth read the article, she decided that a big stack of pancakes might make her feel better. She had mixed the batter and was getting ready to flip the first batch when Jessica appeared, still in her pajamas.

"Yum. What are you making?" Jessica asked, rubbing her eyes sleepily.

"Pancakes," Elizabeth said.

Jessica came over to examine her work. "Make a lot. I'm hungry," she said.

"OK," Elizabeth said. She pointed to the newspaper article. "There's an article about Brooke's disappearance."

"Wait a minute!" Jessica exclaimed. "Coco cancelled her concert? She can't do that!"

Elizabeth turned around and stared at her sister. "I can't believe you," she said. "Brooke could be in serious trouble, her parents are worried sick, and all you can think about is the concert?"

Jessica stared at her feet. "I have front-row seats, Lizzie."

Elizabeth studied her sister's face for a few

moments. She knew something was up. She flipped the pancakes from the pan onto the plate and turned off the burner. She went and sat down directly across from Jessica.

"Jessica, tell me everything you know about Brooke and tell me *now*."

Ten

◇

"I was walking home from Booster practice yesterday afternoon," Jessica began. "Janet called a special cheerleading practice because Winston learned a new cheer from his cousin Alison. It's a really cool cheer. It starts out 'We don't care who's—' "

"*Jessica!*" Elizabeth said in exasperation. "Get to the point!"

"Right," Jessica said. "So I was walking home from practice, and I saw Brooke at the bus stop around the corner from her house. I noticed she was carrying a duffel bag, and she looked awful. Her face was all red and splotchy, and her eyes were swollen. I tried to find out what was wrong, but she didn't want to tell me. Finally she told me she was running away and explained why. I felt really bad for her and I tried to talk her out of it, but she's pretty stubborn. She was determined to run away. So finally I came up with a plan that she agreed to."

"Which was what?" Elizabeth asked impatiently.

"I can't tell you that, but I promise she's fine," Jessica said. "Elizabeth, could you hurry up with those pancakes?"

Elizabeth gave her a withering stare. "Jessica Wakefield, if you don't tell me where Brooke is right now, I'm going to make Mom and Dad a list of every terrible thing you've ever done. And that list will be *long*."

"Geez," Jessica said, trying to look innocent. "I was only asking about those pancakes, because I figure Brooke smells them and she must be getting hungry."

"Brooke is *here*?"

"I convinced her to hide out in the basement until she figures out where to go," Jessica explained. "Of course I was hoping to talk her out of it by then. I promised her I wouldn't tell you, because she thought it would be easier for you if you didn't know."

Elizabeth breathed a sigh of relief. "Jessica, I just don't see how you could have let everybody go on worrying like this. The *police* are looking for Brooke."

"I couldn't betray Brooke, could I?" Jessica argued. "She agreed to come with me only because I swore I wouldn't tell."

Elizabeth went back to the stove and turned the flame on under the frying pan. "I bet Brooke is in serious need of some pancakes."

When Brooke had first woken up in the Wakefields' basement she had panicked. *Where am I?* she wondered frantically. Then she remembered the terrible events of the previous day that had gotten her there.

Her stomach was grumbling from delicious smells that must have been coming from the kitchen, when she heard a noise. She froze. What if Mr. or Mrs. Wakefield found her there? How would she ever explain?

Somebody rapped lightly on the door.

"Brooke," Jessica whispered, opening the door a crack. "It's me—and Elizabeth."

"Elizabeth?" Brooke said. "But Jessica, you promised—"

124

"I know, Brooke, I'm sorry," Jessica said. "But Elizabeth really needs to talk to you."

Jessica and Elizabeth crept into the basement and closed the door behind them. They sat next to Brooke on her sleeping bag.

"Brooke, I know how you feel," Elizabeth began. "I know how awful everything has been for you, but you need to know that your parents are worried sick."

"Look at this," Jessica said, handing the newspaper article to Brooke.

"My mom's going to cancel the concert?" Brooke said. "She can't do that. Even when I try to disappear I make trouble for her career."

"She's not worried about her career. She's worried about *you*," Elizabeth said. "She was furious at Bernice for getting angry at you. She's really sorry about all she's put you through."

"She is?" Brooke said. "I thought she would be so mad at me for telling the paper her real identity that she wouldn't care if I disappeared."

"Brooke, she's not mad at all. She's worried," Elizabeth said.

Brooke paused. "Are you sure?"

"Of course I'm sure. Your parents have the police out looking for you. They're worried something terrible has happened. You've got to call them and tell them you're OK," Elizabeth said.

"But I can't . . . I—"

"Elizabeth's right," Jessica said. "You have to call them."

"Listen, Brooke, there's a huge stack of pancakes waiting for you in the kitchen if you call them," Elizabeth said.

Brooke smiled. "OK, OK, I'll call," she said. "On account of the pancakes."

"Brooke!" her mother gasped. "Where have you been? Are you all right? We've been so worried!"

"I'm fine, Mom," Brooke said. "I didn't mean to make everybody so worried. I just—"

"Where are you, honey?" Mrs. Gray asked. "Can I come get you right away?"

"I'm at Jessica and Elizabeth Wakefield's house," she said, and gave her mother their address.

"I'm on my way," her mother said.

"What did she say?" Jessica asked when Brooke hung up.

"She says she's coming over right away to pick me up."

Jessica's eyes widened. "Coco's coming *here*?" She ran for the kitchen door.

"Where are you going, Jess?" Elizabeth asked.

"To get dressed," Jessica said. "I can't let Coco see the president of Coco Crazy in her pajamas, can I?"

Elizabeth and Brooke laughed.

After Brooke had finished explaining everything to her father and hung up the phone, Elizabeth put a big plate of pancakes in front of her. Brooke couldn't believe how wonderful they tasted. She felt like she hadn't eaten in a week.

A few minutes later she heard a knock on the door. She felt a flutter of nervousness in her stomach.

"Why don't you get it," Elizabeth said. "I'll keep Jessica captive, so you two can have some privacy."

When Brooke opened the door her mom rushed in and gave her a big hug. "I'm so relieved to know you're safe," she said, burying her face in Brooke's hair.

Brooke led her into the living room where they sat down on the sofa.

"Why did you run away?" her mother asked.

"Because I felt so awful about giving our story to the newspaper. Bernice made me realize—"

"Oh, Brooke," her mother said. "Bernice should never have gone to talk to you like that without asking me."

"Bernice said you were furious at me."

Her mother shook her head. "That was wrong of her. I wasn't furious." She took a deep breath. "To tell you the truth I was relieved. I'm so sick of trying to hide who I am, I can't take it anymore. And I can't take you having to hide who you are, either. I'm really sorry I asked you to do that. And I'm sorry I ever let Bernice persuade me to do something I didn't feel in my heart was the right thing to do."

"But aren't you worried about what this is going to do to your career?" Brooke asked. "Bernice says your image is—"

"I've decided if people don't like my music because I'm a mom, that's OK with me," Mrs. Gray interrupted. She smiled. "I've also decided I'm going to get a new agent who is willing to work with me as I am. Someone who realizes how important my family is to me. No career could possibly be more important to me than you and Bobby and Sonya. I'm sorry it had to take an emergency like this for me to see that."

"Oh, Mom," Brooke said, hugging her hard. "Does this mean we can do things together now outside of the hotel like go roller-skating or swimming in the ocean?"

"Absolutely," Mrs. Gray said.

"Mom, you're not going to cancel your concert tonight, are you?"

Mrs. Gray smiled. "Not if you don't want me to."

"I don't."

"So the concert's back on," her mother said, "under one condition."

Brooke looked up nervously. "What?"

"That you promise to come and sit in the front row."

"All right," Brooke promised, and she and her mother laughed.

Eleven
◇

"I can't wait!" Jessica said as she pulled her Coco Crazy T-shirt over her head. She, Elizabeth, Lila, Ellen, Amy, and Mandy were all in Jessica's room getting dressed for the concert. They were all wearing their T-shirts, but Jessica was putting on her complete Coco uniform, including fringed suede jacket, faded jeans, and red cowboy boots.

Everybody laughed when they saw Jessica's finished outfit.

"What's so funny?" Jessica demanded. "I am the president of Coco Crazy, you know. And we're sitting in the front row. I have to look special."

"You look more than special," Mandy said. "You look exactly like Coco."

"Isn't it great that Brooke decided to go to the concert with Colin?" Amy said.

Jessica smiled. "I talked to her on the phone about an hour ago. She was really nervous. We spent at least twenty minutes deciding what she should wear."

"I think they really like each other," Mandy said.

"Are you girls almost ready?" Mr. Wakefield shouted from downstairs.

"We're coming!" Elizabeth shouted back.

"What song do you think she'll play first?" Ellen asked excitedly, applying a last coat of lip gloss.

" 'Hot Coco.' Definitely," Lila said.

"She'll play that last," Ellen argued.

"I think she'll play 'Chocolate Kisses for My Baby' first," Mandy said.

"I wonder if she'll do an encore?" Amy said.

"Of course she'll do an encore. Big stars always do," Ellen said.

"No, they don't," Lila said. "Janet said her brother Joe went to a Johnny Buck concert, and at the end people just kept clapping and clapping, but he'd already left."

"I don't believe that," Jessica said.

Elizabeth laughed. "If you guys don't stop arguing, we'll be lucky if we get there in time for the encore."

"Listen, girls," Mr. Wakefield said as the girls came down the stairs. "I want you to be careful. Stick together, and don't get lost. I'm a little worried about the fact that you don't have a parent chaperon tonight."

"Sure we do, Dad," Jessica said. "Brooke's mom will be there."

The Sweet Valley Arena was packed to the rafters with cheering fans when Coco came out onstage. She looked around and smiled at the crowd.

"Doesn't she look beautiful?" Brooke said in awe.

The cheering became deafening as the band broke into a fast, loud rendition of "Chocolate Kisses for My Baby." As Coco sang and danced around the stage, the whole crowd stood up and danced and cheered.

Brooke felt a chill of excitement run through her entire body.

"She's an incredible singer," Colin yelled above the noise.

"I know," Brooke shouted back. She grinned. "She's my mom."

After the first set of songs, the arena quieted down and Coco brought the microphone to the edge of the stage.

"I have a very special person to introduce to you tonight," she said, and the audience became even quieter, straining to listen.

"As some of you might have read in the papers," Coco said with a smile, "I lead a double life. Onstage, I'm a performer. At home, I'm a mom." She reached her hand down to Brooke and pulled her onstage. Brooke felt her mother's arm around her waist, holding her tight, as she looked out over the sea of faces.

"Say hello to my beautiful daughter!" Coco called. Brooke smiled as the cheering got louder and louder.

"It was perfect," Jessica said as she helped Elizabeth set the table Sunday night.

"Totally perfect," Elizabeth agreed.

"Wasn't it great going backstage?" Jessica said.

"It was awesome," Elizabeth said.

"Brooke looked so happy."

"I think everything is going to be fine with her mother," Elizabeth added.

"It wouldn't be so bad having a rock star for a mother," Jessica said. "Maybe we can get mom started on the tambourine or something."

Elizabeth laughed.

"You know, Lizzie, life is so great. Everything with Brooke is settled, last night was the best night of my life, Aunt Helen is coming this week, Aaron still hasn't asked for his suede jacket back. . . . What more could I want?"

"I hate to rain on your parade, Jess," Elizabeth said, "but I think Mom and Dad finally discussed the subject of our punishment for having had a party while they were gone."

Jessica made a face. "Thanks for reminding me. I was hoping they had forgotten about it, but then Mom found a huge dried-up glob of mustard on the dining room window this morning and I think it kind of refreshed her memory."

Elizabeth frowned. "I hope it's not too horrible."

A few minutes later the Wakefields were sitting around the table, and Mr. Wakefield cleared his throat. "As you kids know, your mother and I were very disappointed to hear that you had a number of friends over with no adult supervision while we were gone," he said.

Steven, Jessica, and Elizabeth all nodded.

"We also felt that you kids were right to come right out and confess what you had done. You could have gotten away with it scot-free, but you felt you needed to tell us."

Steven gave Jessica a wry look.

"That showed real maturity, and your mother and I are proud of you," Mr. Wakefield continued. "For that reason we've decided not to ground you or take away any privileges."

Jessica returned Steven's look. She was all ready to start cheering when her father cleared his throat again.

"We were also so impressed with the way you cleaned up the entire house yourselves—with the exception of a few stray cold cuts—that we'd like you to do the same thing in preparation for Aunt Helen's visit this week."

Steven's jaw dropped. "We have to clean up the whole house?"

Mrs. Wakefield gave him a knowing look. "Yes. Believe me, it could have been a lot worse."

"I just talked to Aunt Helen today and she said she's coming a day *early*," Mr. Wakefield added cheerily. He looked around at three frowning faces. "Don't be too sad. Aunt Helen said to tell you that she got a big surprise for each of you."

Jessica's ears perked up. "A surprise? A big surprise?"

What does Aunt Helen have in store for the Wakefield kids? Find out in Sweet Valley Twins and Friends No. 56, **THE WAKEFIELDS STRIKE IT RICH.**

We hope you enjoyed reading this book. If you would like to receive further information about available titles in the Bantam series, just write to the address below, with your name and address: Kim Prior, Bantam Books, 61–63 Uxbridge Road, Ealing, London W5 5SA.

If you live in Australia or New Zealand and would like more information about the series, please write to:

Sally Porter
Transworld Publishers
(Australia) Pty Ltd
15–23 Helles Avenue
Moorebank
NSW 2170
AUSTRALIA

Kiri Martin
Transworld Publishers (NZ) Ltd
3 William Pickering Drive
Albany
Auckland
NEW ZEALAND

All Bantam and Young Adult books are available at your bookshop or newsagent, or can be ordered from the following address: Corgi/Bantam Books, Cash Sales Department, PO Box 11, Falmouth, Cornwall, TR10 9EN.

Please list the title(s) you would like, and send together with a cheque or postal order to cover the cost of the book(s) plus postage and packing charges of £1.00 for one book, £1.50 for two books, and an additional 30p for each subsequent book ordered to a maximum of £3.00 for seven or more books.

(The above applies only to readers in the UK, and BFPO)

Overseas customers (including Eire), please allow £2.00 for postage and packing for the first book, an additional £1.00 for a second book, and 50p for each subsequent title ordered.

created by FRANCINE PASCAL

Jessica and Elizabeth Wakefield have had lots of adventures in *Sweet Valley High* and *Sweet Valley Twins* . . .

Now read about the twins at age seven! All the fun that comes with being seven is part of *Sweet Valley Kids*. Read them all!

THE SADDLE CLUB

Bonnie Bryant

Share the thrills and spills of three girls drawn together by their special love of horses in this adventurous series.

1. HORSE CRAZY
2. HORSE SHY
3. HORSE SENSE
4. HORSE POWER
5. TRAIL MATES
6. DUDE RANCH
7. HORSE PLAY
8. HORSE SHOW
9. HOOF BEAT
10. RIDING CAMP
11. HORSE WISE
12. RODEO RIDER
13. STARLIGHT CHRISTMAS
14. SEA SHORE
15. TEAM PLAY
16. HORSE GAMES
17. HORSENAPPED
18. PACK TRIP
19. STAR RIDER
20. SNOW RIDE
21. RACE HORSE

Forthcoming:

22. FOX HUNT
23. HORSE TROUBLE